CW01185031

© Catherine Coles, 2020

All Rights Reserved including the right of reproduction in whole or in part in any form.

Inspired Press Limited

www.catherinecoles.com

ISBN: 9798555404183

This is a work of fiction. Names, characters, places and incidents either are the products of the author's imagination or are used fictitiously. Any resemblance to actual persons living or dead, business, companies, events or locales, is entirely coincidental.

Editor – Sara Miller

Cover Artist – Sally Clements

MURDER AT THE VILLAGE FETE

A 1920s cozy mystery

A Tommy & Evelyn Christie
Mystery - Book 2

CATHERINE COLES

About the Author

Catherine Coles has written stories since the day she could form sentences, she can barely believe that making things up in her head classes as work!!

Catherine lives in the north east of England where she shares her home with her children and two spoiled dogs who have no idea they are not human!

Catherine's Cozy Mysteries

Murder at the Manor
Murder at the Village Fete
Murder in the Churchyard

Catherine's Website

www.catherinecoles.com

"Everything will be okay in the end. If it's not okay, it's not the end."
– John Lennon

CONTENTS

Chapter One 11
Chapter Two 24
Chapter Three 38
Chapter Four 51
Chapter Five 64
Chapter Six 78
Chapter Seven 91
Chapter Eight 105
Chapter Nine 119
Chapter Ten 132
Chapter Eleven 146
Chapter Twelve 156
MURDER IN THE CHURCHYARD 168
COMING JANUARY 2021 168
A Note from Catherine 169

Cast of Characters

Main Characters

Tommy Christie – The 7th Earl of Northmoor, former policeman
Evelyn Christie – Policewoman during the Great War, Tommy's wife

The Family

Lady Emily Christie – Tommy's great aunt
Horace Hamilton – Evelyn's father
Martha Hamilton – Evelyn's mother
Millicent Wilder - Evelyn's sister
Reg Wilder - Millicent's husband

The Guests

Robert Billingham – MP for Northmoor & East
Edith Billingham – Robert's wife
Frederick Barrow – Horace's long-time friend
Margaret Barrow - Frederick's wife
Sidney Payne – Horace's long-time friend
Ann Payne – Sidney's wife
Theodore Mainwaring - The village doctor
Isolde Newley – The new village schoolteacher

The Staff

Wilfred Malton - The butler
Phyllis Chapman - The housekeeper
Mary O'Connell - The cook
Walter Davies - Charles's valet
Frank Douglas - Eddie's valet & First Footman
Arthur Brown - Second Footman

Gladys Ferriby - Lady Emily's lady's maid
Doris - Evelyn's maid
Nora - The kitchen maid
Joe Naylor - Gardener

Villagers

George Hughes – The owner of the village pub, the Dog & Duck
Annie Hughes – George's wife
Albert - The butcher's boy, Nora's beau
Geoffrey Beckett - Villager

Others

Detective Inspector Andrews – Senior detective
Detective Sergeant Montgomery – Junior detective
Ernest Franklin – journalist covering the village fete for his paper, the York Times

Chapter One

North Yorkshire, England – Autumn 1921

"No, Davey!" Evelyn Christie called after her mischievous young puppy.

He did not stop, let alone turn around and come back. Even as she chased him down the gravel driveway of her new home, Hessleham Hall, Evelyn knew well that running after puppies was not becoming behaviour for a countess.

In actual fact, it wasn't socially acceptable for *any* lady, let alone one who was desperately trying to prove to her house full of guests she wasn't hopelessly out of her depth.

Margaret Barrow, the wife of one of her father's oldest friends, had been scathing since she had arrived to stay for the weekend. In less than twenty-four hours, she had complained about her room, the food and, more bizarrely, the weather.

Of course, it had to be that particular guest's fur stole that Davey now had in his mouth as he abruptly changed course and galloped towards the lawn at the side of the house in the carefree way only puppies can.

Evelyn paused, leaning forward and placing her hands on her knees. She tried desperately to catch her breath as she drew level with the corner of the large imposing building that now belonged to her husband, Tommy. If she followed Davey, any of her guests who happened to look out of a window would see her.

"Help is on its way!"

Evelyn straightened and looked behind her at the sound of the friendly voice. Still breathless, she gasped out her thanks.

Isolde Newley, the new teacher at the local village school, placed a reassuring hand on Evelyn's back. "Your maid has gone to the kitchen for sausages to lure the little fellow in."

"Mrs Barrow's stole will be ruined." Evelyn stared after Davey, the garment bouncing along the grass behind him.

"It's quite ghastly," Isolde said, wrinkling her nose in distaste. "Davey is doing us quite a service by running away with it so we do not have to see it across the dinner table any longer."

Evelyn laughed. "You're right. It is particularly grim, isn't it? However, Mrs Barrow seems very proud of it."

"Mrs Barrow is a very discourteous individual."

Evelyn smiled at her guest. It was hard to believe she had only met the other woman the previous afternoon. In their brief acquaintance, the two women had learned they had many things in common—not least their dislike for rude middle-aged women.

"I don't know what more I can do to make her feel comfortable in my home."

Isolde shrugged. "I believe she is one of those types of women who is only happy when she has something to complain about. I don't think there's anything *anyone* could do to make her happy."

"And now her prized possession is covered in puppy drool, grass stains and probably mud," Evelyn moaned. "Whatever will I do?"

"Here comes the cavalry." Isolde pointed as Doris approached at a fast clip.

"Oh, Mrs Christie...ma'am..." Doris panted. "I'm so very sorry. I don't know how he got out."

"It really isn't your fault, Doris. He's a very naughty puppy. I believe he must sense when there's a door open somewhere and heads straight for it." Evelyn gestured towards the package in her maid's hands. "What do you have there?"

Doris had coloured a bright pink that Evelyn thought had little to do with the exertion of running from the kitchen to the gardens, and more because she had slipped up and referred to Evelyn in the old way.

She herself was not the only one who was finding it difficult adjusting to life at Hessleham Hall and all the new rules and ways of doing things. One slight mistake in how she was addressed wasn't something she was going to spend a single moment worrying about. And neither should Doris.

"Sausages, Lady Northmoor," Doris responded, looking over at Isolde as though wanting their guest to know that she was aware of how to properly speak to her mistress. "I will run after Davey from this direction. Perhaps you and Miss Newley can casually stroll through the gardens from the other direction?"

"We shall head him off whilst looking as though we are simply taking a leisurely walk." Evelyn nodded.

"Much better that if anyone should get caught chasing through the grounds, it be me and not yourself." Doris giggled nervously.

"You are an absolute pet, Doris. Thank you."

"She's been with you a long time," Isolde commented as Doris raced past the edge of the house after Davey. It was not a question.

"Since Tommy and I married, and we had our first home in the village." Evelyn linked arms with Isolde as they walked back past the entrance of the house and towards the opposite side. "Doris was with me through the war, and those awful months when I didn't know what had happened to Tommy when he was reported missing in action."

"That does rather explain your closeness."

"We are all still adjusting." The events that had led to Tommy and Evelyn becoming the new Lord and Lady Northmoor were very recent, but they had happened before Isolde had started working at the village school at the beginning of September. "Tommy works way too hard. Partly because his uncle before him, the previous Lord Northmoor, was not awfully good at keeping up with the estate but mostly because he wants to prove himself."

"I read about what happened in the newspaper." Isolde nodded. "It was quite the scandal. Talk in York was all about what they called the 'country squire murders'."

Evelyn felt very comfortable talking to Isolde, as though they had known each other for much longer than a single day. She had a way of chatting away that was not gossipy and that felt to Evelyn as though the other woman was really interested in what she had to say.

"Did you know the detectives sent from York originally arrested Tommy?"

"What?" Isolde exclaimed, her green eyes wide with interest. "Goodness, how perfectly dreadful. He didn't do it, of course?"

"No, Tommy doesn't have that sort of evil in him. He's a very ordinary fellow. Well, we both are, actually, despite the situation we've found ourselves in." Evelyn spread her left arm wide to encompass the enormous house that was now her home. "We both rather miss the cosy little suppers we had in the parlour in our little cottage. That was much more 'us' than the stuffy formal dinners we have here."

"Instead, you now spend hours working out a menu, where guests should sleep, and such like?"

"Indeed." Evelyn nodded. "Our cook and housekeeper are wonderful and do so much of it, only needing me to approve their suggestions. I couldn't refuse when my father asked if he could invite his old chums and their wives down for the weekend, but I would rather have had a smaller number as it is our first time receiving overnight guests."

"I really could stay in the village, it would be no problem getting home on an evening. I am sure Dr Mainwaring…"

"I didn't mean to suggest that you are a burden. Quite the opposite. You are the only person of my age staying. I absolutely insist that you do not go back to the village." Evelyn shot a sidelong look at Isolde. "Though if you wanted to spend more time with the doctor…"

Isolde turned and grinned, not a bit embarrassed at Evelyn's suggestion that she may be romantically interested in Dr Mainwaring. "Do I make it so very obvious? He's quite dashing, but extremely quiet. He barely responds when I talk to him."

"I think he's overcome," Evelyn answered. "Teddy is naturally a reserved man, though he and Tommy have become friendly lately. I expect he is simply struck dumb when you speak to him. You're very beautiful."

Isolde was a tall, curvy redhead and Evelyn was certain she commanded the attention of men in every room she entered without making a single effort.

They stopped walking then, and Isolde looked at Evelyn with tears in her eyes. "It's been a very long time since anyone has said something like that to me and I've been even slightly inclined to believe their words."

The sudden change in the other woman confused Evelyn, and she wasn't sure what to say next. Her new friend had, until that moment, seemed very self assured and happy. Evelyn couldn't help but wonder what had happened in Isolde's past.

She shook her head slightly. The last time she had spent too much time concerning herself with other people's lives and their secrets had been that summer when she and Tommy had solved the murders of Tommy's uncle and cousin.

That kind of excitement could jolly well stay in the past. Evelyn was much too busy learning how to be a proper lady to get mixed up in that kind of adventure again.

***

"I should imagine Davey thought he was improving the item's quality," Aunt Em commented. "We cannot blame the animal for thinking it was his duty to remove that hideous thing from the house."

"Aunt Em!" Evelyn tried, and failed, to smother a smile at the old lady's words. "Shh! Mrs Barrow will hear you."

"I do not care one single jot if she does," Tommy's great aunt retorted. "It cannot possibly be the first time someone has remarked on how truly revolting that garment is."

"Doris and Mrs Chapman rubbed the stains out and Doris had to dry it in front of the fire after she retrieved it from Davey." Evelyn hid her giggle behind her pre-dinner glass of gin and tonic. "We had to bribe him with sausages just to get him to drop it."

Em looked at where Margaret Barrow stood with her husband next to the fireplace, the fur stole proudly draped around her shoulders. "It would have been better for everyone if he had dumped it in the river, never to be seen again."

Margaret chose that particular moment to look over and caught Evelyn and Em staring at her prize possession. She walked over to them. "Lady Northmoor, Lady Emily, I see you are both admiring my beautiful stole. Would you like a closer look?"

Evelyn opened her mouth to answer, then closed it again. From the corner of her eye she could see Isolde with a handkerchief held up to her mouth, obviously hiding her mirth.

"I have seen nothing like it in my life before."

"Indeed, Lady Emily, it is exquisite, isn't it?"

Aunt Em's face did not flicker as she replied. "I have absolutely no words."

Fortunately, Malton announced dinner, and the group moved through to the dining room. Evelyn looked around the table anxiously, hoping the seating arrangement she had spent hours agonising over would work. She had grown up as the daughter of a prominent member of parliament, but believed arranging guests around a dinner table involved more political machinations than her father had ever utilised in his entire career.

Her parents, Horace and Martha Hamilton, were joined at Hessleham Hall by his oldest friends—Frederick Barrow and Sidney Payne with their wives, Margaret and Ann. Her father had also pressed Evelyn to invite the current member of parliament for the constituency of Northmoor & East, Robert Billingham and his wife Edith, to stay at Hessleham Hall for the weekend.

Robert had been asked to officially open the annual village garden fete the next morning. Traditionally, the event took place in July, but the previous owner of Hessleham Hall had not allowed the villagers to use the manor house's grounds for the fete that summer.

However, Evelyn's sister, Millicent, was on the village committee and had used powers of persuasion that would put any politician to shame to get Evelyn to agree that she and Tommy would host the event in the autumn.

It had been a very great risk as the summers in their part of northeast England were hit and miss in terms of the weather. Autumn usually brought endless days of rain and dreary grey skies. Although the last couple of days had been chilly, fat white clouds had been pushed along the clear blue sky by a relatively light sea breeze. Evelyn hoped the dry weather would continue to hold out for at least another day as the event was so important to Milly.

That evening, she had seated herself between Robert Billingham and Theodore Mainwaring, the village doctor. As the guest of honour, it was only proper that the member of parliament was seated next to her. Evelyn had known him since she was a child but had not seen him for many years. Thankfully, she was saved from having to find safe topics of conversation as he had not looked her way once. Instead, he was fervently discussing something with Ann Payne in rather hushed tones.

Relieved, Evelyn turned to the doctor. "How are things in the village, Dr Mainwaring? I have not had time to walk down as often as I would like recently."

"Oh, much the same as always, Lady Northmoor," he answered, stroking his luxurious moustache. Evelyn had noticed he did that when he felt uncomfortable. "Nothing ever stays the same, except perhaps for a doctor."

"How do you mean?"

"The world may change around us and the medical instruments I use may improve, but ultimately there will always be the joy of new birth and the despair of death." His eyes flicked away from hers as he looked down the table to where Isolde sat between Frederick Barrow and Sidney Payne.

"The excitement of new love is something to celebrate, is it not?"

Dr Mainwaring used his thumb and forefinger to smooth the whiskers on either side of his mouth. "Should one be so lucky, I am sure that would be a source of great happiness."

"And yet you sound anything but happy," Evelyn mused.

"Let us not pretend that I am an extroverted and amusing chap that people look forward to sitting next to at dinner," the doctor said somewhat morosely. "I know quite well that I am rather dull and talk excessively about subjects that do not interest ladies."

Evelyn thought carefully before she answered. Whilst her immediate impulse was to deny what the doctor said, she did not wish to be untruthful. "I know that there is a certain lady who would very much like to get to know you better. Perhaps, in order to feel more confident when speaking to such a lady, you would like to learn how to talk more confidently on a range of fascinating subjects?"

Dr Mainwaring looked up from his empty soup bowl, interest flaring to life in his eyes. "Do you think…that is…can one learn how to be engaging?"

"Certainly that is possible." Evelyn nodded. "My understanding is that you have become friendly with my husband?"

"He is a smashing fellow." The doctor nodded. "I would very much like to be more like him."

"My point is not that you need to be more like Tommy," Evelyn said. "But that you are able to talk to him and simply be yourself?"

"I suppose that is correct." Dr Mainwaring looked confused, as though he could not follow Evelyn's thought process at all.

"You are talking to me now without reservation." Evelyn took a sip of wine. "I think that is because you are not trying to impress me."

"That may be correct." The doctor looked again towards Isolde, who was talking animatedly to Frederick Barrow. His expression turned morose. "I would give anything for her to look so enthralled when speaking to me."

"Let us help you achieve that aim." She smiled at her dinner companion. "Tommy and I will spend some time with you tomorrow and after we are finished with you, ladies will be clamouring to spend more time with you."

"I would be happy with just the one lady," he said with feeling. "But the fete is tomorrow, you and Tommy will be surely be too busy."

"My sister is in charge of the fete," Evelyn explained. "I am needed only to provide whatever she needs to make it a success. I would be pleased to give you whatever assistance I can."

"I would be very grateful, Lady Northmoor."

"That is settled, then. Tomorrow, after breakfast, we shall begin your lessons."

Evelyn had never attempted to play Cupid before, but after the horrors of the war and Spanish flu, spreading a little happiness would be a very welcome relief.

***

The following morning, before breakfast, Tommy and Evelyn took both dogs for a walk in the grounds of Hessleham Hall. There wouldn't be much opportunity for the dogs to be exercised later that day as the fete was due to begin after lunch.

Nancy danced around Evelyn's feet, teasing Davey, who could not be trusted to run loose like the older dog. He strained on his lead, little yelps of pure puppy delight the only sounds on the air.

The grass was damp with dew, the weak autumnal sun doing its best to break through the thick cloud cover. Evelyn loved this time of day. She was just a young wife walking her dogs. Later, she would be Lady Northmoor, and the entire village would be watching and gossiping about her every move.

Not that she resented everything about her new position. There were some parts of being Lady Northmoor that were very enjoyable. For example, she could approve her sister's request that the villagers hold their annual fete on the grounds of Hessleham Hall. She also now served on many committees that helped people less fortunate than herself. Tommy had also indulged her hobby of raising pedigree Gordon Setters by purchasing Davey from her mother for Evelyn's recent birthday.

The good definitely outweighed the bad. Evelyn reminded herself of that when she spent hours with her staff agreeing upon which rooms to assign guests and completing menus for their stay. Such things she found tedious, but they were a necessary duty.

She had found the food served the evening before quite delicious, but after dinner Mrs Barrow had complained to anyone that would listen about the quality of the salmon mousse. Evelyn was finding it increasingly difficult not to take the other woman's criticisms personally.

"Will you speak to Teddy after breakfast?" Evelyn pulled her hat lower on her head as the chilly wind coming off the North Sea whipped around her ears.

"I shall endeavour to find out whether your matchmaking efforts are something he definitely wishes to encourage and take part in."

Evelyn pulled a face. "He completely agreed last night."

"Perhaps the poor fellow simply acquiesced, so he could eat his meal in peace."

"Thomas Christie!" Evelyn cried in mock horror. "I resent the implication that Teddy did not agree to my plan of his own free will."

Tommy stopped walking and put a hand on Evelyn's arm to stop her footsteps. "Are you certain that Miss Newley likes Teddy? I should hate for us to meddle, and raise his hopes, only for her to dash them."

"She told me so herself." Evelyn reached up and kissed her husband. "Oh Tommy, wouldn't it be just wonderful if those two could be as happy as we are?"

Tommy wrapped an arm around Evelyn as they continued their walk. "I shouldn't think anyone could be as happy as we are together."

"Nancy!" she called as the animal raced away towards the stream at the end of the lawn. Davey pulled on his lead, yapping excitedly as he tried to follow the older dog.

"What is she doing?" Tommy dropped his arm from around Evelyn's shoulders and hurried after Nancy.

The dog sat on the river bank, her head thrown back, as she howled into the early morning air. Her behaviour was very unusual. Gordon Setters were gundogs, and Evelyn had trained Nancy to work with her when they attended shoots. She had never seen her dog behave in such an odd manner.

The sound the animal made was long, low and mournful. Fear tickled its way down Evelyn's spine. She tried to tell herself she was being ridiculous and there was nothing to be afraid of, but she couldn't shake the feeling of foreboding. Something was terribly wrong.

If the noise Nancy was making wasn't enough, the stiff set of Tommy's shoulders when he caught up with the dog convinced Evelyn she was right to be afraid.

Evelyn caught hold of Tommy's hand. "What is it?"

Davey's tail drooped and hung between his legs, and he finally stopped pulling on his leash. Instead, he positioned himself behind both Nancy and his mistress as the older dog continued her plaintive wail.

Lying face down as the stream gently trickled around him was a man. The water flowing away from his body was tinged pink, and a large kitchen knife was sticking out of his back.

There could be no doubt that Robert Billingham, the Member of Parliament for Northmoor & East, was most assuredly dead.

Chapter Two

Tommy walked back into the drawing room and sat beside his wife on the sofa. "Detective Inspector Andrews is on his way from York."

"I cannot believe this is happening again." Evelyn took a sip of tea.

"It's extraordinary how people keep getting themselves killed," Aunt Em agreed. "And the timing is incredibly inconvenient."

"I don't suppose Mr Billingham had much choice about when he met his end." Tommy looked at his great aunt with a mild look of reproach on his face. "Are we certain that is who it was, darling?"

"Positive." Evelyn nodded. "The body was the correct size and build, but it was his hair that clinched it."

Tommy turned a quizzical glance her way, but Aunt Em knew exactly what Evelyn meant. "It is entirely too dark for a man his age."

"It doesn't look real." Evelyn reached forward and gently placed her teacup on the table in front of her.

"That's because it's not, dear." Aunt Em patted Evelyn's knee. "It is clearly a hairpiece."

"How do you ladies know these things?" Tommy wondered.

"I take the time to study people." His aunt told him. "If you had spent as many years as I have observing mankind, you may well be as knowledgeable as I am."

Evelyn suppressed a chuckle. It would not do for someone to walk past the room and hear merriment coming from within. "You were correct about the mild weather holding."

"There was no doubt. I have been telling you for weeks that the weather would be fine enough for the fete to be held in early October. Though I cannot imagine the police will allow it to take place given there is a lunatic on the loose."

"Poor Milly will be so upset." Evelyn referred to her sister, Millicent, who was the complete opposite of their mother. Milly planned everything in her life down to the very last detail and made sure her every planned action was performed to perfection—which she had done with the village fete. Unless it had something to do with her dogs, Evelyn was certain Martha Hamilton had never organised anything in her entire life.

"Your sister will recover herself quickly, I'm sure." Evelyn's father spoke from the doorway. "However, I would suggest that Mrs Billingham may take somewhat longer to recover herself."

"Of course." Evelyn flushed. "I intended no disrespect."

"Billingham was a rather hard fellow to like," Horace Hamilton said. "But his family will still mourn his passing."

"Has he now been positively identified?" Tommy asked his father-in-law.

"The local police constable took Edith outside, and she has confirmed it," Horace referred to Robert Billingham's wife, a stout, no-nonsense woman who had steadfastly supported her husband through the highs and lows of his political career. Including the infamous Carpelli scandal.

"How well did you know him?" Tommy asked his father-in-law.

Evelyn recognised the interested look on her husband's face. She had seen it that summer when his uncle, and then his cousin, had been killed.

Tommy had taken to his new role as Lord Northmoor with the same energy, enthusiasm, and passion that made him the special man that he was. However, Evelyn knew how desperately he missed the work he had done in the police force prior to the war.

In those days, they had lived in their little cottage in the village. Tommy had his job and Evelyn had helped her mother with the dogs. When he came home in an evening, he entertained Evelyn with stories of the different cases he was working on. His face had shown the same excitement as it did now—they had been presented with a puzzle, and her husband was keen to use his detecting skills to solve it.

"I have known him for many years," Horace replied carefully.

"And it seems to me that you did not like him?" Tommy pressed.

Horace thought for a moment before responding. "He had a rather vexatious manner. Jolly difficult to explain exactly what made him so unpleasant."

"Please try, sir?"

"He seemed to believe it was acceptable to be rude because of his station in life. I think he thought being a Member of Parliament meant he was somehow better than others."

Now was most definitely not the time to voice her opinion that her father himself had a very similar manner. How odd that he was able to see that in his peer, but not in himself. Horace Hamilton had enjoyed an illustrious career as a politician until he retired and his lifelong friend, Robert Billingham, had put himself forward as the new candidate for Northmoor & East.

"Despite your feelings, you were very insistent that Evelyn and I host the Billinghams and your other friends this weekend. May I ask why that was?"

Horace's gaze snapped to Tommy's as though he was only just realising that his mild-mannered son-in-law was a former detective who was clearly asking him questions for a reason. "May *I* ask why that matters?"

"Your friend is dead, sir," Tommy responded bluntly. "I am wondering if there could possibly be a connection between his untimely death and the weekend gathering that you yourself orchestrated. I am certain that will be the first question Detective Inspector Andrews will ask when he arrives from York."

"The Carpelli scandal." Horace looked at Evelyn, and for the first time in her life she could see shame and embarrassment in her father's eyes.

"You were cleared of any wrongdoing." Evelyn looked between her father and Tommy. "Why are you going over old ground?"

"It has always bothered me how the media found out that the way some contracts were awarded during the war was not entirely legitimate."

"That's putting it mildly," Evelyn retorted. "I believe the Carpelli scandal involved money exchanging hands, so a particular company was given a huge government contract?"

"That is correct."

"Obviously I was out of the country when this happened," Tommy said. "But I recollect those implicated were yourself, Robert Billingham, Sidney Payne and Frederick Barrow?"

Tommy did not need to point out the obvious. Whilst he was abroad trying to save his country, there were many unscrupulous businessmen attempting to line their own pockets and profit from the war. Horace Hamilton had been accused of being one of those men.

"Why does what happened three years ago matter so much now?" Aunt Em's eyes narrowed as she looked at Evelyn's father.

"I received a letter." Horace passed a hand over his eyes, his expression now troubled. "It suggested that the newspapers are sniffing around this story and fresh evidence has been uncovered. When I telephoned Billingham, Payne and Barrow they had all received similar correspondence."

"Who was the sender of the letters?" Tommy asked.

"That's just it," Horace said. "They were typewritten, with no signature. I have no idea who may have sent them. None of us do."

"And now Billingham has been killed." Tommy got up from the sofa and walked over to the window and looked out over the lawn in the direction of the stream where they had found the body. "We must assume that he knew something."

"Must we?"

"Absolutely." Evelyn held up a hand and took hold of one finger. "Reason number one: Why was he out so early that morning? Two: Was he meeting someone? Three: Could he have been killed by the person he was meeting? Four: Or could he have been killed to prevent him from divulging information to the person he was meeting?"

Tommy took over. "Evelyn is correct. She has come up with four plausible possibilities in a very short time. No doubt we will come up with many more as we uncover more information."

"You must get sleuthing immediately, darlings," Aunt Em said, an unmistakable glint of excitement in her blue eyes. "I cannot wait to see Detective Inspector Andrews turn that peculiar shade of purple again when you uncover the murderer before him."

***

"What can I do?" Evelyn asked as she washed her hands at the sink in the kitchen.

Mary O'Connell, Hessleham Hall's cook, had now had two months to get accustomed to the lady of the house dropping into her domain, wanting to help out. She still commented to Mrs Chapman that it was highly irregular, but it was a halfhearted effort at propriety. The truth was, her mistress was a very capable cook and her sense of fun brightened what could be a very stressful environment.

"I've made shortbread," the cook responded in her charming Irish lilt. "You could cut it into rounds and fill the trays I have ready?"

"Of course." Evelyn rolled up her sleeves and pulled the bowl of shortbread dough towards her. She floured the surface in front of her. "Where is Nora?"

"She's fetching lemons. I know it's not summer, but I thought pitchers of lemonade as well as pots of tea for the fete this afternoon would be nice."

"Very nice, Mrs O'Connell, thank you."

"I hear that woman was uncomplimentary about my salmon mousse?"

Evelyn sighed as she rolled out the dough. She had hoped to avoid this conversation, but she should've known Margaret Barrow's grumbles would reach the kitchen. At first, it had surprised her that word travelled so quickly in such an enormous house but she knew now that was the way of things. A question could be asked in the drawing room, and the entire staff would know what it was before an answer could be given.

"I'm afraid very little agrees with Mrs Barrow."

"Is that a polite way of saying she is just downright mean?" Nora asked as she returned to the kitchen. "You have a very polite way of saying things, Lady Northmoor."

"Thank you, Nora." Evelyn smiled at the kitchen maid. "Even when other people are very rude, I still believe it is important to treat everyone the way you would wish to be treated yourself."

Nora giggled. "That's exactly what I mean. You've just suggested Mrs Barrow is very rude. But you haven't actually said that, have you?"

"Indeed." Evelyn used the pastry cutter to form biscuits. "It would be very wrong of me, especially in front of staff, to suggest that a guest is anything but gracious."

"Even if they moaned about every meal you slaved over for them?" the cook grumbled.

"Even if they are the type of person who has clearly had their taste buds removed," Evelyn said firmly, then smiled at the older lady. "Your salmon mousse was exquisite."

"Thank you, Lady Northmoor."

"She's blushing!" Nora pointed at the cook. "See how you've made her blush."

"Pshaw!" Mrs O'Connell flapped a hand in their direction. "Get on with your work and I'll pour us all a nice cup of tea to drink while we work."

"That'll wet me whistle," Nora said, looking at Evelyn. "I'll need it because you're going to ask me what I know, aren't you?"

"You're very perceptive, Nora." Evelyn pushed a tray full of shaped dough ready to go into the oven and pulled an empty tray toward her as she started the process all over again. "I hope you've got lots to tell me."

"As it happens." Nora began cutting the lemons into halves. "I have."

Evelyn hid a smile at the young girl's enthusiasm. She was even learning the art of dramatic pauses.

"Does this tale begin with the arrival of the butcher's boy?"

As expected, Nora flushed bright red. It was well known within the household that Nora had a crush on the butcher's delivery boy, Albert, and it seemed like the lad was just as keen on Nora.

"Yes, Lady Northmoor, it certainly does."

"Do go on,"

"I'm surprised you get any work done, girl, the amount of time you gasbag with that boy." Mrs O'Connell put steaming cups of tea on the table in front of where they were working.

Her words might have sounded harsh had Evelyn not been fully aware that the cook usually treated Albert to a slice of freshly made bread covered in homemade jam and a cup of tea before he cycled back down to the village to continue his deliveries.

"When Albert arrived this morning, he said he had seen someone sneaking out of the house and it looked a bit strange to him."

"Sneaking?"

"Well, that's what was strange," Nora explained. "He said I should go and see for myself." The girl shot a hesitant look at the cook, as though she would be harshly reprimanded for leaving the kitchen. "I was only gone a minute."

Evelyn stopped what she was doing and looked at Nora, fully engrossed in the maid's story. "What did you see?"

"Well, it was just like Albert said." She took a sip of tea and licked her lips. "Someone was walking away from the house, but they kept looking back over their shoulder. As though they was worried someone would see them."

"Do you know who it was?"

"They were too far away." Nora shrugged. "They had on a brown overcoat and a hat. Like the one

Lord Northmoor wears when he goes into the village."

"It was a man then?"

"I should think so." Nora cut the lemon on the chopping board and then put the two halves into a bowl Mrs O'Connell had passed her. "But it wasn't that fellow who died."

"How can you be sure?"

"He was tall and walked upright, like Lord Northmoor. The person Albert and I saw was shuffling along with their head down, as if they were up to no good. Just like how that poacher, Geoffrey Beckett, used to walk when he was coming down the lane."

Nora's comparisons were very good and showed that she had put thought into what she had seen, knowing Evelyn would want to know precisely what she had observed.

"To be clear, Nora," Evelyn said as she finished cutting the dough. "This was *before* breakfast?"

Nora looked confused. "Of course, Lady Northmoor. It couldn't have been after breakfast because we were waiting for Albert to arrive with the sausages and bacon to make a start."

"Very good." Evelyn drank her tea. "As usual, Nora, you have been very useful. Thank you for being so observant. I shall write to the butcher so he is fully aware of how happy Lord Northmoor and I am with Albert's service."

"Albert would be ever so pleased. He might even get a raise."

"Let us hope if that happens, he uses some of his extra money to buy his favourite girl something nice." Evelyn looked pointedly at the scarlet ribbon in Nora's hair.

Red was not a colour that the maid would've bought herself. She was a sensible girl and would certainly have thought it too frivolous a shade. It was definitely the sort of thing a man would buy to impress a girl.

***

"I don't know whose idea it was to hold a summer fete in autumn." Evelyn watched as the gardener cleared yet more leaves from the lawn as she walked the grounds of Hessleham Hall with her sister, Millicent Wilder.

"You know very well it was mine," Milly replied.

Evelyn returned the gardener's wave. "Poor Joe Naylor looks exhausted."

"Do you think it will all be worth it?" Milly asked.

"I've told all the staff to continue preparations for the fete as though it is going ahead as planned," Evelyn said. "I have absolutely no idea if Detective Inspector Andrews will give permission. Tommy is very worried too. He would never forgive himself if someone was hurt during the fete."

"I would imagine a knife wielding madman would find it difficult to blend in."

Evelyn raised her eyebrows at her sister's tart tone. "I can't imagine the villain would try something in the middle of a busy event. But then, crowds of people could provide a rather decent diversion. And whoever said it was a madman?"

"Well, it is usually a man, isn't it?" Milly wrinkled her nose in distaste. "Women don't go around stabbing people, do they? It's so very violent."

"I think it's more likely to be a man," Evelyn agreed. "And you're right, women don't tend to use such aggressive methods of killing."

"It could be simply anyone. I wonder what Robert Billingham did wrong?" Milly shuddered. "Maybe we should call it off."

Evelyn thought about what her father had said. "Perhaps he did nothing. He could have been killed because of something he knew."

"Let's not talk about it anymore," Milly said. "It quite unnerves me. I know you like this sort of thing, but I don't. Not at all."

"Will Reg bring the children up later?"

"Yes." Milly brightened immediately at the mention of her family. "Can you believe Reg has the entire weekend off duty?"

Milly's husband was a doctor at the local hospital and worked long hours. Evelyn thought how nice it would be for her sister and her family to enjoy an afternoon of fun. "The children will surely enjoy…"

"Perhaps by next year's fete, you may have a child of your own." Milly's words were casual enough, but Evelyn didn't miss the pointed look her sister gave her. "The boys would love a cousin to play games with."

"You could just give them a little brother yourself." Evelyn immediately regretted her abrupt tone. It wasn't Milly's fault that she was wary of having children.

"Actually," Milly said as she put a hand on her stomach. "Reg and I are rather hoping for a girl this time."

Evelyn stopped walking and threw her arms around her sister. "Congratulations! That is wonderful news. Just what I needed to cheer me up after this morning's shock."

Milly kissed her sister's cheek and then held her at arm's length. "Me providing this family with another offspring does not get you off the hook."

Evelyn looked up at the big house behind her sister. It wasn't yet a contentious subject between herself and Tommy, but she knew if many more years passed without her being ready to have a child, it would begin to cause issues between them.

"I'm not ready."

"What about Tommy?"

Evelyn smiled wryly. "I think he was born ready."

"Suddenly inheriting this house and the title hasn't made him more ready?"

"No." Evelyn shook her head. "Tommy would have been happy to have children when we first married."

"What are you so afraid of?"

The stark question, without superfluous words to lessen the impact of the simple phrase caught Evelyn off guard. She and Tommy had spoken about her reluctance to be a mother, of course, and he understood her reasons. "Mostly making a horrible hash of it and causing my children to be as wretchedly unhappy as we were."

"Do my children look miserable?" Milly asked sternly.

"Of course not," Evelyn said. "But I don't think anyone from the outside looking in would have thought we were particularly sad children and yet we were."

Milly looked lost in thought but Evelyn knew her sister well enough to be aware she was simply picking her next words very carefully. "Yes, we were and now that I am a mother I am aware of what does not work. I may not do things perfectly, and I sometimes get things wrong, but never from lack of effort."

"Your children are very lucky to have you."

"And your children will be very lucky to have you," Milly squeezed Evelyn's hands in her own.

"Tommy says the same thing."

"Tommy is a very wise man. You will not hear me say this very often, but on this subject, perhaps you should listen to your husband."

"As you listen to yours?"

"Reg is an absolute pet," Milly said. "Over the years he has learned to say 'yes, dear' to most of what I say. But even mild mannered Reg knows when it is time to tell me no."

Evelyn couldn't imagine Milly's quiet, studious husband refusing his wife a single thing, he utterly adored her. "When was the last time Reg didn't agree with you?"

"This morning, actually." Milly grinned. "I told Reg I intended to wear my salmon pink dress."

"And what did Reg tell you?"

"Reg told me I would be an absolute fool if I wore that dress because it was meant for summer. I told him it complimented my hair. And he told me it was no good my hair and dress looking lovely if my nose was running because I was freezing cold." Milly shrugged. "And so I put my favourite dress back into the wardrobe because on that occasion, Reg was quite correct."

Evelyn joined her sister in laughter. It was a very sweet story, but despite Milly and Tommy's assurances she was still not ready to have children though it was certainly getting harder to remind herself of exactly why that was.

"Hey, there!" A young man called as he made his way across the grass towards the sisters.

Evelyn looked at her sister, certain Milly's shocked expression was mirrored on her own.

When the stranger caught up with them, Milly assumed a haughty look that Aunt Em would have been proud of. "Are you addressing us?"

"You're Mrs Wilder aren't you? Her what's in charge of the fete?"

"I am Mrs Reginald Wilder." Milly's voice was cold enough to freeze the entire North Sea. "And this is my sister, Lady Northmoor."

"Pleased to meet you both, I'm sure." He performed a curious movement that was somewhere between a bow and a curtsey. "I'm

Ernest Franklin, from the York Times I've been sent to cover the fete for my paper."

"To cover the fete?" Evelyn repeated. "But it's just a simple village fete. I cannot think of anything you could write that your readers would possibly be interested in."

"That may well have been true, Mrs Northmoor, but that was before the murder!"

"Young man." Milly stared at Ernest who was much younger up close than he had seemed when he hailed them across the lawn. "My sister is properly addressed as Lady Northmoor and you are intruding on a private conversation."

The last thing that Tommy would want was stories in the local newspaper about yet another body being found at Hessleham Hall. The paper could, of course, report the murder but Evelyn was determined they would not have a story to go with it.

She focussed on sounding as grand and commanding as Aunt Em as she drew back her shoulders. "If you do not leave my property immediately, I shall set the dogs on you. Now be off with you."

Ernest turned around and hurried off in the direction from which he had arrived.

"The dogs?" Milly was laughing so hard, tears streamed from her eyes.

"He wasn't to know Nancy would've licked him all over and Davey would have stolen that preposterous mustard coloured handkerchief and run off with it."

Evelyn's gaze turned serious as Ernest stopped running and waited for the car that was making its way up the drive to stop in front of the house. Detective Inspector Andrews had arrived.

Chapter Three

"I must say, this is very inconvenient." Margaret Barrow's strident voice rose up above the buzz of gentle conversation in the drawing room.

Detective Inspector Andrews looked at the woman with an arched eyebrow. "And why is that, Madam?"

"You have us all crammed in this room like a herd of animals and your underling has said we are not to leave."

"My Detective Sergeant is quite correct," he said with exaggerated patience. "A murder has taken place, and it is my job to solve it. Preferably before anyone else gets hurt."

"Anyone else?" Margaret echoed.

"Indeed, madam." He nodded, then looked over to Tommy. "Perhaps, My Lord, you could introduce me to everyone?"

"Of course." Tommy rose from the sofa where he had been sitting with Evelyn. "You know my wife and my aunt?"

"Ladies." Detective Inspector Andrews nodded politely towards Evelyn and Aunt Em.

"He's trying to do his job correctly this time," Aunt Em whispered. "Instead of sitting back and waiting for you and Tommy to solve it as he did last time."

"How nice to see you again, Detective Inspector," Evelyn said, doing her best to ignore Aunt Em. "Though it's under very unfortunate circumstances."

Tommy indicated Horace. "This is my wife's father, Sir Horace Hamilton."

The policeman moved over to Evelyn's father and shook his hand. He had learned from the last time he was at Hessleham Hall that this was a man his superiors would want him to treat with the utmost respect. "I've heard a lot about you, Sir Horace. Is your wife not with you?"

"She went back down to the village after breakfast," Horace mumbled, looking slightly embarrassed. "To see to the dogs, you know."

"I believe the instructions I left with the butler were that no one should leave the house?"

The question didn't seem to be aimed at anyone in particular. When his father-in-law did not answer, Tommy stepped in. "Indeed, you did. Mrs Hamilton was very concerned about her dogs. She has popped home to see to them, and she will return shortly."

"I..."

"Is my mother-in-law a suspect?" Tommy asked, a steely undertone to his words.

"I do not believe so," the detective answered. "However, it is protocol in situations such as this that all of those present at the crime scene stay in the same place."

"None of us were present during the crime," Tommy said quickly, capitalising on the error in the policeman's words. "And I am sure that you will agree, it would have been possible for practically anyone to enter the grounds and kill poor Mr Billingham."

"He's making a mess of things already," Aunt Em said with undisguised glee. "Tommy will put him right."

"You do not believe it was someone who is staying here at the house?"

"I think it is most likely to be someone who is staying here," Tommy said smoothly. "However, I think it would be prudent not to dismiss the notion of someone coming up from the village to commit the heinous crime."

"I have not arrived at any conclusions at this early stage."

"I am very pleased to hear it." Tommy smiled innocently. "In that case, there can't be an issue with my mother-in-law being absent for a couple of hours. Now, moving on."

Aunt Em gave a quite audible giggle of delight as Tommy finished introducing the guests—one retired politician, two currently serving and their wives, and the local Member of Parliament's widow. "He's turning that funny colour again."

"Sssh," Evelyn admonished, though Aunt Em was right. Detective Inspector Andrews looked very ill at ease in the company of so many important men.

"Perhaps you will remember Dr Mainwaring, our esteemed village doctor?" Tommy was now saying.

The detective nodded. "Doctor."

"And last but most definitely not least, this is Isolde Newley, the village schoolteacher."

"Newley?" he repeated, brow furrowing. "Now where have I heard that name recently?"

"It's not an entirely uncommon name," Isolde said as she moved from where she had been standing next to the fireplace and shook the policeman's hand. "In fact, it's very commonplace where I'm from."

"Which is?" Detective Inspector Andrews answered immediately, then seemed to look at the woman whose hand he was enthusiastically shaking.

"New Earswick." The response, when it came, was delayed and delivered almost as a question rather than as an answer.

Evelyn's eyes met Tommy's, and she knew her husband was thinking the same thing as she was. Whilst Detective Inspector Andrews may have just accepted Isolde's reply because he was in awe of her beauty, they were both aware that Evelyn's new friend had just told a very blatant lie.

***

"I didn't think for a moment he would allow the fete to go ahead," Isolde commented as she helped Evelyn arrange the stall she had agreed to take care of. "Mrs O'Connell has outdone herself, this is a quite marvellous creation."

Evelyn propped a sign asking villagers to 'guess the weight of the cake' against the plate displaying the enormous strawberry gateau. "I think the doctor has a bit of competition from Detective Inspector Andrews for your affections. He looked rather taken with you."

So taken, in fact, that he quite forgot the suspicions he had voiced when he first heard her name.

Evelyn, however, had not forgotten how the detective's brow had creased as he tried to remember where and when he had recently heard the surname 'Newley'.

She had already added this snippet of information to her mental list of things that required investigating. It was possible Aunt Em knew someone in the village Isolde claimed to be from. Or perhaps one of the Hessleham Hall servants had friends, family or other acquaintances around the New Earswick area of York.

The chances of there being more than one Isolde Newley born in the York area in the last twenty-five years or so was surely very slim.

Isolde looked down and fiddled with the bunting that had been placed around the plain wooden table and transformed it to a stand suitable for Mrs O'Connell's culinary masterpiece. "The detective does not interest me at all."

"How unfortunate for him, when he seemed so very interested in you," Evelyn said, not able to help saying exactly what she thought.

Isolde looked at her with a small, sad little smile that made Evelyn feel instantly contrite. She looked over toward the front of the house. "People have started to arrive. How exciting!"

Contrary to her words, Isolde looked forlorn and as though she wished she could be anywhere but on the grounds of Hessleham Hall surrounded by villagers wanting to guess the weight of cakes, have a turn on the coconut shy or have tea and cake with their friends.

Only yesterday Evelyn had believed she would be firm friends with the woman in front of her, but today she realised how very little one could get to know another person in less than twenty-four hours.

Aunt Em sat in a chair under an awning, though the older woman was right, there would be no rain that day. Her legs were covered by a heavy blanket and she rested a saucer on her lap.

"What a shame there is no band this year," Em commented as Evelyn reached her side. "We usually have a jolly band that helps to keep spirits up. Everything has a rather subdued feel."

"Do you think that's because of the murder, that there's an undercurrent that is making everyone feel uneasy?"

"Perhaps those of us at the house, dear." Em nodded. "But not the villagers. I can't imagine there's one of them that has given Robert

Billingham another thought. Your father was quite right. He wasn't a very nice man."

"Milly says we didn't have enough people who can play an instrument to form a band. Isn't that awful?"

Em looked up across the lawn at the throng of people. "There wasn't a single house in the village that the war left unscathed. But to look at people now, you wouldn't know they had a care in the world."

"Yet you're right about there being a rather downcast feel about things."

"I don't think it comes from them, it comes from within us." Em tapped a hand against her chest. "We experienced murder close at hand only a few short months ago, and now we must do so again. We saw the very worst that people can do to each other, and I believe that we both know we are going to see the blackness that lives within some people once more."

"Oh, Aunt Em." To her horror, Evelyn found herself having to blink back tears. "I think you're right."

Em looked up at Evelyn and patted her arm. "Now is most definitely not the time to feel sad about what has happened, or what is to come. It is a time for action. You find that husband of yours and you must both get busy finding out who the murderer is."

"Oh no," Evelyn muttered.

"Who is that youth?" Em asked, following Evelyn's gaze.

"He is a reporter," Evelyn said. "Milly and I met him earlier. I threatened to set the dogs on him if he didn't leave."

"You are a constant source of new amusement." Em chuckled. "There are times when I quite forget how new to all of this you are given you have taken to it so very well."

"Have I?" Evelyn asked earnestly. "I often feel like I am making a complete mess of everything."

"In my vast experience," Aunt Em said with the grand tone in her voice that Evelyn so admired. "I believe that if your guests are complaining, but not moving on, then you are doing an excellent job."

"I'm not sure I understand."

"We do not have time to discuss this at any length. Now, stop fishing for compliments and escape while you can. Send that boy to me."

Evelyn almost felt sorry for the reporter. "My husband's aunt, Lady Emily Christie, would be pleased to help you with your article."

"Would she?" he asked doubtfully.

"Absolutely," Evelyn replied, indicating where Aunt Em sat. "She is waiting for you now. There is nothing she doesn't know about the village and she is very keen that you get all the details you need for the article you are writing about our little fete."

"Who is that?" Tommy asked as he reached Evelyn's side.

"Ernest Franklin, the reporter I told you about earlier."

"The one you met earlier when you were conspiring with your sister to nominate me to open the fete?"

"The very same." Evelyn squeezed his hand. "May I just say how very gallantly you cut the ribbon. I don't think the scissors have ever been wielded with such aplomb by anyone before in the history of the Hessleham village fete."

"I felt like such a fool."

Evelyn knew her husband wasn't comfortable with that type of thing, but Milly had begged her to convince Tommy to step into the breach left by Robert Billingham's death.

"I'm sorry, darling, but as I said you looked quite magnificent."

"You are aware I will plot and wreak my revenge?"

"I shall look forward to it."

***

"There is a small window of opportunity before dinner," Tommy said to his friend, Teddy Mainwaring, as he drew him into the billiard room.

"For what, old fellow?"

"My wife informs me that there is a young lady staying at the house who has caught your eye."

Teddy nodded. "Lady Northmoor very kindly suggested that she would help me speak to Miss Newley in a manner that would not send her to sleep."

Tommy clapped a hand on his friend's back. "I'm sure your conversational skills are not as bad as all that."

The doctor nodded. "It is quite dreadful, I assure you."

"Then let us help you." Evelyn clapped her hands together as the men entered the room and closed the door behind them.

"But we do need you to keep something in mind whilst you're talking to Miss Newley." Tommy frowned at Evelyn. This part of their plan felt very underhanded to him, even though he had been the one to suggest it to Evelyn.

"Of course," Teddy agreed amiably, as was his nature.

"We do not believe that Miss Newley is from the village of New Earswick as she claimed earlier when she spoke with Detective Inspector Andrews."

"Why do you think that she was untruthful?"

"He seemed to recognise her name." Tommy shook his head. "Well, maybe not *her* name exactly, but her surname. It wasn't *Isolde* that piqued his interest, but Newley. It may be as simple as a family member she is ashamed of."

"But it may be something more important," Evelyn chipped in.

"I recognise this look that you both have." Dr Mainwaring looked between his friend and Evelyn. "You are investigating the death of Billingham?"

"We must." Tommy shrugged. "It happened whilst he was a guest at our home. We would be doing him a great disservice if we did not uncover the perpetrator."

"I need not remind you that the police are here to do just that. Andrews and his sidekick?"

"You need not remind us," Tommy said. "But sadly, they could not find out the information they needed to apprehend the person who murdered my uncle and my cousin."

"We very much believe that people tend to tell us things they would not feel comfortable telling the police." Evelyn added as she leaned forward in the high-backed leather armchair in which she was seated.

"And you think Miss Newley is hiding something that she will not tell the police and may not tell you two either?" Teddy stroked the corners of his moustache. "And you want me to use the conversational skills you are going to teach me to find out what she's hiding?"

"I think that may be a touch optimistic for the twenty minutes we have." Tommy poured himself a drink and raised the bottle in a silent offer to the doctor. "It is, however, possible that your conversations may stray to the subject of her family and her childhood naturally. We would ask you to let us know if anything of interest should arise."

Having nodded his agreement to a drink before dinner, Dr Mainwaring took the tumbler from Tommy. "It feels a little like spying on the lady to me."

"It's for a very good cause," Evelyn said. "We wouldn't ask if we did not feel it was necessary."

"Indeed." Teddy took a sip of the whiskey and soda.

"I have taken the liberty to alter the seating arrangement at dinner somewhat. You will be seated next to Miss Newley this evening." Evelyn smiled in what she hoped was an encouraging way, all the while feeling like she was completely betraying her new friend.

It was possible Miss Newley had nothing to hide, and she had either misspoken as she was nervous around the police—some people were. Or, much less possibly in Evelyn's opinion, she and Tommy had misread the situation. They had discussed the chances of that, but neither of them had given that option much credence. Both of them were exceptionally good at reading people, and they both had exactly the same opinion.

"We had better move along with my tuition." Teddy glanced at the grandfather clock in the corner of the room. "We are running short on time."

"Tell me how you would normally speak to a lady," Evelyn suggested. "How would you ordinarily begin a conversation?"

"Perhaps I might comment on the quality of the food," Dr Mainwaring stroked his whiskers with one hand while he thought. "Sometimes the weather, if it had been a particularly pleasant day. Or even a very bad one. Lots of rain and the sort."

"Right." Evelyn nodded. "We have plenty to work with."

"We do?" Surprise was evident in the doctor's words.

"Yes," she agreed smoothly. "There are plenty of ways that we can improve your conversational skills. Currently, you are discussing subjects that will give very limited responses. A lady may compliment the food or agree with you about the weather. At this point, the exchange ends."

"Absolutely." Dr Mainwaring nodded enthusiastically. "What am I doing wrong?"

"You have chosen 'safe' subjects, but ones that allow very few new avenues of dialogue. You must consider asking a lady what her interests are, if she has family. Perhaps talk to her about subjects on which you are well versed."

"You like horses, Teddy. You could ask a lady if she likes to ride. If the answer is in the affirmative, you could then enquire whether she may like to go out riding with you."

"We couldn't go alone, though, that wouldn't do."

"No, of course not," Tommy agreed with infinite patience. "That's where you must use a little machination."

"Oh, I wouldn't want to be dishonest." Teddy shook his head. "That is not for me. I shouldn't wish to trick a lady."

"Not at all, old man." Tommy finished his drink. This was much harder than he had anticipated. "On an occasion such as this, you would tell the lady that a group of friends were intending to go out for a ride the next day."

"What if such an outing was not planned?"

"Then you plan one."

"I see," Teddy nodded slowly. "I invite a lady on an event that I then organise because I know it will be something that she will enjoy?"

"By jove, you've got it!"

"The only trickery involved is finding a subject that both interests a lady and she is happy to discuss with you." Evelyn added.

"Out of interest." Teddy looked between his friends. "How did Tommy win your attention, Lady Northmoor?"

It didn't matter how many times Evelyn had asked Teddy to call her Evelyn in private, he still insisted on her formal title though he didn't use Tommy's. "He didn't use any social niceties on me, I am afraid."

"No." Tommy laughed. "I threatened to arrest her."

"You did not!"

The doctor laughed and Evelyn could see then what Isolde found so attractive. When he forgot to be serious and staid, which were commendable attributes for a doctor, he was a very handsome man.

"He most certainly did."

"She was climbing in through a window and I thought she may intend on committing a criminal offence and so I told her if she did not get down from the ladder immediately I would be forced to follow her up and arrest her there and then."

"Goodness." Teddy looked at Evelyn in awe. "What were you doing up a ladder?"

"It was my own home," Evelyn explained. "My mother had locked the doors thinking Milly and I were home. She's very forgetful, you know. I was intending on climbing in through a window and then letting Milly in."

"You were not able to raise your mother by knocking on the door?"

"She was in an outbuilding at the back of the house with one of her dogs. She had fallen asleep and did not hear us." Evelyn shook her head wryly, laughing at the memory.

"Would you have arrested her?" Teddy looked over at Tommy.

"I knew exactly who she was and that the window she was attempting to climb through was her own home."

"Why on earth would you tell her that you were going to arrest her then?" Teddy asked, puzzled.

"I had admired Evelyn for such a long time, and that was the first opportunity I had to strike up a conversation with her. When she got down from the ladder, I said I wouldn't arrest her if she went to a village dance with me."

"And, of course," Evelyn carried on the story. "I thought he was incredibly dashing in his policeman's uniform. And I had waited simply *ages* for him to ask me to go dancing with him."

"So you see," Tommy said. "It is all a sort of game. Evelyn knew I was following her around plucking up the courage to speak to her. In the same way, you already know Isolde would like to get to know you better because she has told Evelyn. It is now your move."

The doctor finished his drink and placed his empty glass on a side table. "Then I must dress for dinner and prepare to make my move."

Chapter Four

After dinner, the guests all gathered in the drawing room. Detective Inspector Andrews and his colleague had taken their meal in the library where they had set up their base of operations.

Edith Billingham sat alone on one of the long sofas next to the fireplace. Her ample body was encased in a plain black wool dress that Evelyn could imagine no one would have packed for a weekend away with friends. However, as far as garments went for mourning, it was perfect.

Since her husband had been found that morning, Evelyn had had little opportunity to observe the older woman, so she sat opposite Edith. There were no obvious signs of distress on the face of the wife of the dead man. She did not look as though she had been weeping, her nose was not red as it would have been had she blown it many times.

"I thought the fish a little dry," Margaret Barrow said loudly, finishing her gin and tonic and signalling for another.

"She is certainly drinking as though her throat is incredibly dry," Aunt Em commented from her seat next to Evelyn. "She may find she can taste her food better if she drinks less alcohol."

"I do wish you would stop your constant carping," Edith said without looking at her friend. "It's very tiresome."

The quiet hum of conversation stopped at the widow's words and everyone turned to look at her. "What?" she snapped. "I am simply saying what you all think."

"I am sure Margaret meant no offense," Ann Payne spoke up.

"I certainly did not take any," Evelyn offered, feeling as though she needed to diffuse the situation. She didn't like the look that had passed between Edith and Margaret—as though there were secrets only they knew, and the keeping of them was festering like a sore.

"You didn't cook the meal," Edith turned to Evelyn, who was dismayed to see real venom in the other woman's face. "It is your cook who should take offence, should any be taken."

"Perhaps," Aunt Em said, her voice low but clear in the crowded room. "We should all take a moment to compose ourselves and remember that we are guests in Lord and Lady Northmoor's home and behave accordingly."

"Bravo." Ann Payne nodded in agreement.

"Oh, shut up!" Edith exploded. "How respectful were you of the owners of this home when you spent the entire meal last night whispering to my husband, you painted trollop? And shall we talk of how I caught you sneaking around the corridors last night?"

"I was searching for someone to ask for a glass of water," Ann stumbled over her words.

"Ordinary house guests would pull their bell!" Edith's tone was now strident, and her face had flushed with anger. "I am aware you were searching for my husband's room."

"Now see here," Ann's husband, Sidney, spoke up. "That's uncalled for, Edith. We all know that you are very upset, but you should not turn on your friends when you shall need them for support."

Margaret got up from her seat and went over to Edith, sitting beside her, and putting an arm around her shoulders. "You poor thing."

"Do get off me." Edith shrugged away Margaret's arm and edged away from her on the sofa. "And keep that unspeakably foul, smelly thing away from me."

"My fur does not smell." Margaret's lip quivered as though she was going to cry. "It was *very* expensive."

"Oh, do let's all calm down and remember that we are friends," Ann suggested. "We shouldn't let those beastly letters come between us."

"What letters would those be?" Detective Inspector Andrews spoke from the open doorway.

"We all got one," Margaret said, desperate to ingratiate herself with someone.

"We did not all get one," Edith contradicted. "Our husbands all received a letter. It is nothing to do with us."

"Perhaps Mrs Payne is right and we should all take a breath and settle down." The policeman strode into the room and sat in one of the vacant chairs next to the fireplace. "Now, Mrs Billingham, can you please tell me about the letter your husband received?"

Edith stared at Ann for a long moment before she turned to the detective to answer his question. "It was a few weeks ago. Robert received a letter saying additional evidence had been uncovered, the press were aware of this, and moves were being made to reopen the enquiry into the Carpelli scandal."

"And you received a similar communication?" Detective Inspector Andrews looked to Frederick Barrow, who nodded, and then to Sidney Payne.

"I believed the missive to be a precursor to blackmail."

"Why would you think that, Mr Payne?"

"If someone were aware of new facts that would break open the Carpelli scandal, they would simply go to the papers and demand their price. The person has written to us four individuals because we are perceived to be rich men and might pay more than Fleet Street were willing to."

"I can see the logic behind your reasoning." The detective looked over at Evelyn's father. "Did you also receive one of these letters?"

"I did," Horace spoke stiffly.

"Do you still have it?"

"It is at home with the rest of my papers."

Detective Inspector Andrews looked around the room before looking back at Horace. "Then perhaps you can telephone your wife, who does not seem to have returned, and ask her to locate the letter. I shall then send Montgomery into the village in the car to collect both your wife and the note."

"I would rather accompany Montgomery and retrieve the letter myself."

"As you wish." The detective's gaze did not waver, he seemed much less in awe of Horace than he had earlier that day. "But please return with your wife and the item I have requested. I do not wish to be in a position where I must take further action against you for impeding my investigation."

Horace blew out a breath, and for a moment, Evelyn thought he was going to have one of his infamous tantrums—one that would be as bad as Edith's outburst. "I shall leave now."

Evelyn tried to make sense of the additional information that she had learned that evening, but found it hard to piece the different facts together.

She knew Carpelli Industrial Limited was a company contracted to provide supplies for the army to help with the war effort.

The suggestion that morning was that an unknown person had paid a member of parliament a large sum of money to give Carpelli the contract, and it had implicated all four friends in this transaction. An investigation after the war had found no evidence of wrongdoing by any of the four men, or by the company, but something had clearly happened because Robert Billingham was dead and those around him were all acting as though they may very well be next.

***

The following morning, Evelyn went back to visit the kitchen staff. The previous evening had left her feeling unsure of her father's guilt or innocence. When news of the scandal had broken, she had never had a moment's doubt her father hadn't participated or had knowledge of the bribe paid to secure the contract. Now she wasn't so sure, and that uncertainty drove her need to find Robert's murderer. She must get to the bottom of this mystery and not allow her father's name to be dragged through the mud once more.

"Good morning, everyone," she said brightly.

It wouldn't do for the staff to think there was anything wrong with her. She broke many of the rules of propriety with her staff, but she believed part of her role as Lady Northmoor was to keep her employees healthy and happy whilst they worked.

"Good morning, Lady Northmoor!" Nora called from the sink where she was elbow deep in soapy water, no doubt washing that morning's breakfast dishes.

"I don't really have anything you can get stuck into this morning, I'm afraid." Mary O'Connell looked around her well ordered kitchen as though she could summon up dough ready for kneading, biscuits that needed cutting out, or a cake requiring decoration.

"Perhaps there are some vegetables I can peel?"

"I must draw the line, My Lady." The cook shook her head decisively. "Preparing food on the kitchen table is one thing, cleaning and peeling dirty vegetables is quite another. Imagine you pouring afternoon tea with filthy fingernails. I would be so ashamed."

Evelyn smiled. "I *do* know how to wash my hands thoroughly, Mrs O'Connell, but I take your point."

"I can certainly pour you a nice cup of tea." The old lady's Irish lilt had softened, and she looked at Evelyn for a long moment. "You look exhausted, if you don't mind my saying so. Have my seat here by the fire and perhaps a strong cuppa will revive your spirits."

So much for not letting the staff see that the murder had troubled her! Mrs O'Connell had seen straight through her in an instant. "I am a little anxious about what happened to poor Mr Billingham. I do not believe that I slept quite as soundly as normal."

Mrs O'Connell fussed around Evelyn. Her brusque and abrupt tone was a flimsy cover for her caring, maternal nature. She reminded Evelyn of the cook her mother had used in their home when she was a girl. The kindly lady had been more of a parent to Evelyn and Milly than their own mother ever had. She had listened with infinite patience to their worries and concerns before giving advice, which was liberally dosed with dollops of common sense.

The cook gave Evelyn a large mug of steaming tea instead of the usual delicate cup and saucer she was accustomed to. "Get that down you and you will be feeling right as rain in no time."

"Thank you." Evelyn nodded, then bowed her head as, completely unbidden, tears filled her eyes. Now was absolutely not the time to feel sorry for herself because her mother had been emotionally absent and left Evelyn needing more as she grew up. The war and the Spanish Flu epidemic had left children with no mother at all. Self pity was definitely not required when one was living in a beautiful stately home with a husband who utterly adored her.

"I expect you want to know about the knife?"

"Yes." Evelyn pulled herself together and raised her chin. "I most certainly do."

"The detective came down to the kitchen yesterday afternoon with the ghastly implement."

"Ghastly?"

Mrs O'Connell pulled a face, glanced over at Nora, then lowered her voice. "It was still covered in the gentleman's blood."

"Oh, I see," Evelyn said. "How particularly gruesome."

"Indeed." Mrs O'Connell folded her arms under her ample bosom as though to show the sight had not bothered her in the least, but Evelyn could see by the rapid rising and falling of the other woman's chest that reliving the memory upset her.

"I suppose he wanted to know if the knife was missing from your kitchen?"

"He did."

The cook's eyes suddenly would not meet Evelyn's and she knew what the answer would be before she asked, but she still needed to ask it. "And was it missing from this kitchen?"

"Yes, My Lady."

Mrs O'Connell couldn't look more ashamed than if she had taken the knife herself and plunged it into Robert Billingham's back. "You have no idea who may have taken it?"

"I don't, My Lady. Oh, I'm right glad you don't think I could have had anything to do with this dreadful business. As you know, I'm a God fearing woman. If I knew who had done such a dastardly deed here in your home I would tell you straight away. And I told that detective fellow the same."

"I did not think, even for a single moment, that you or your staff could have had anything to do with what happened." Evelyn reached over and put a hand on the cook's arm. "Lord Northmoor and I know how very hard you all work to keep us both happy and we are truly grateful for how easy everyone has made it for us to adjust to our new roles."

The cook reached out and picked up her own mug of tea, wrapping her hands around it and taking a fortifying sip. She took a moment before she looked back at Evelyn. "Serving you and Lord Northmoor is a pleasure, especially compared to that what we were used to. I don't want to speak ill of the dead, but the previous Lord Northmoor and Master Eddie were very difficult to please."

"If you feel able, could you please describe the knife to me?"

"I can do better than that, Lady Northmoor. I can show you one almost exactly the same."

Evelyn nodded. "That would be very helpful."

Mrs O'Connell got up and went to fetch the knife. Nora looked at her curiously, but didn't make any comment. She returned and carefully handed the knife to Evelyn. "The one that went missing is similar. I prefer the handle on this one, so use it more often."

"When did you last use the one that was used to kill Mr Billingham? Can you remember?"

"The police asked the very same thing." Mrs O'Connell frowned. "I will have to tell you the same thing I told him, I really cannot recall. As I say, I favoured this one, so I don't even remember when I last saw the other one."

"But it is definitely from this kitchen?" Evelyn asked, wanting to be absolutely certain that someone had taken a knife from the house, and not arrived already prepared to kill.

"Oh, yes." The cook nodded, certainty in both her voice and the vigorous nodding of her head. "We have always used the same bladesmith. If you look carefully, you can see his mark on the bottom of the blade close to the handle."

Evelyn peered at the knife in the area Mrs O'Connell had told her about. She could indeed see the craftsman's insignia. "Was the detective able to see this same mark on the other knife?"

"He wasn't certain, because of the blood, but he thought he could make out the bladesmith's mark."

"Well, I think that settles that then, don't you?"

"Yes indeed, Lady Northmoor."

"Someone has crept downstairs, possibly after dinner when you had all gone to bed, and taken a knife in readiness for the act they had planned to perpetrate the very next morning."

"It fair makes my back tickle with fear, I don't mind saying."

"Mine too," Evelyn agreed. "It is very unsettling. I believe I shall go and find my husband and tell him all that I have found out. Thank you, Mrs O'Connell. Thank you very much."

***

"In here, if you don't mind, My Lord." Detective Inspector Andrews stood at the door to the billiard room looking as though he had been standing there waiting for Tommy to walk past.

"Not at all," Tommy said easily. "Have you been waiting for me for long?"

"How do you mean?" The detective asked suspiciously.

"I was thinking that if you need to speak to me, as the owner of the house, instead of standing in doorways in the hope I will pass by some time soon it would be wise to send one of my staff to find me."

"I wanted to speak to you quite urgently."

Tommy frowned. "Which makes even less sense. Why would you not send for me or send your colleague to locate me?"

Montgomery wasn't in the room and Tommy didn't remember seeing him since the previous evening when he had taken Horace down to the village to bring back both his wife and the letter he had received.

The other man shrugged. "I don't suppose it matters that I tell you I was hoping to speak with you before you had an opportunity to speak with Lady Northmoor."

Tommy sat in one of the high-backed leather armchairs in front of the windows that looked out across the lawn. "Why would you wish to speak to me before I spoke to my wife?"

"You must reason with her."

"With Evelyn?" Tommy was quite mystified.

"There is a madman on the loose," he clarified. "One who went into the kitchen of your own house and took a knife that he then used to kill one of your guests. Four of your guests, including the dead man, have received anonymous letters."

"We are very aware of the unfortunate events of the last day," Tommy said, a cool note creeping into his voice.

"And I." Andrews thumped himself on the chest with one fist. "As a serving police officer, have a duty to not only locate the killer but to prevent him from committing another terrible act."

"You do think there's a good chance there will be another murder if the person is not caught?"

"Well, don't you?" he retorted, then seemed to remember that he was attempting to take control. "I am aware that you were a police detective, and that this is your home, but I must beg of you, Lord Northmoor, please let me do my job."

"I have absolutely no intention of preventing you doing just that, old fellow." Tommy crossed his legs and relaxed into the chair. "Though I still cannot understand why you wish me to 'reason' with my wife, as you so eloquently put it."

"Lady Northmoor is currently in the kitchen."

"My wife often visits the kitchen." He spread his arms out. "Of our own home."

"It is surely highly irregular for a woman of her standing to go downstairs." The detective flushed. He was unsure of how large houses such as Hessleham Hall were run, but certain the lady of the house would not make it a habit to visit her staff below stairs.

"That is very true." Tommy nodded. "However, my wife is not at all like most other wives. You remember those scones you were served for afternoon tea last time you were here?"

"Indeed I do, very light and…"

"My wife made those." Tommy was aware a note of pride had entered his voice. "In the kitchen of our home. She likes to bake. In fact, it's very possible she is downstairs making the bread rolls we will serve with the soup we will serve for dinner this evening."

"But…but why?"

"Why when we have staff to do these things for us?"

"Yes." The detective nodded, looking perplexed.

"Because she enjoys to bake. We are both aware that there are things women of a certain class should not do. However, we are both in agreement that if it is acceptable for me to go out on to the estate to work with Partridge, our estate manager, then it should be acceptable for Evelyn to go work with our house staff if she wishes to."

"It seems a very modern arrangement," Andrews commented, still looking unconvinced.

"You are not married yourself?"

"I am not."

"Well, when you are, do remember that the first rule of a harmonious and successful marriage is to keep your wife happy. If my wife wishes to bake and it makes her happy, I am happy for her to do that as often as she wishes."

"I don't suppose she would talk to the staff whilst she was baking about things they may have seen?" At Tommy's frown, the detective clarified. "Say, for instance, whether the cook had recognised the knife I showed her yesterday as being one that belonged to her kitchen equipment?"

"Are we talking about the knife that killed Billingham?" Tommy sat forward in his seat. This discussion was finally getting interesting.

"We are indeed."

"I'm afraid I cannot give you a very authoritative answer about the topics ladies discuss when they are baking."

"But it is possible the cook will have mentioned, or Lady Northmoor, may have asked about the murder weapon?"

"Of course it is possible." Tommy chuckled. "It is also possible they spoke about the rising cost of eggs, whether the butcher's boy will pluck up the courage to ask the kitchen maid out to a dance or whether there will be snow for Christmas."

"The cost of eggs is rising?"

Tommy had no idea whether hens were laying frequently or what in fact affected the price of the eggs they did or did not lay. "I'm certain I heard Evelyn talking about that the other day. But then ladies talk about so many things, don't they?"

The detective seemed to finally remember why he had asked to speak to Tommy. "I must ask that neither you nor Lady Northmoor attempt to investigate this matter. It is a very serious crime, the most serious of all, and amateurs should not allow themselves to impede important police work."

"I can tell you honestly that we will not attempt to investigate, and neither shall we get in the way of your investigation." Tommy rose from his chair and put out his hand.

The detective grasped the offered hand and shook it. "Then we are agreed."

"Absolutely." Tommy nodded. "No attempting. And no getting in the way."

Chapter Five

"I had understood from Detective Inspector Andrews that he is in complete charge of this incident." Horace lifted his cigar case from the inside pocket of his jacket. "Ladies, do either of you mind if I smoke?"

"No, Father, go ahead."

"As you wish, dear," Martha Hamilton said. She had returned from the village with her husband, as requested by the detective.

Evelyn smiled to herself at her mother's words. She really couldn't remember a time when her mother hadn't said those four words in response to a query from her father. That was her answer regardless of what Horace asked her. Evelyn had long since stopped wondering whether her mother actually listened to Horace's questions.

"Will you take one?" Horace offered the cigars to Tommy.

"Not for me, thank you." Tommy moved over to a side table and removed an ashtray, putting it on the table beside Horace. "The detective is quite correct. He is the officer in charge of finding out who killed Billingham."

Horace lit his cigar and blew out a plume of smoke into the air of the billiard room before continuing. "Then why do you have us in here to answer your questions?"

"We're family." Tommy extended his arms, palms face up. "Can we not take a few minutes to catch up privately away from the rest of the guests?"

Horace peered at Tommy over the top of his glasses. "I don't believe you."

"We promised not to attempt to investigate and not to get in the fellow's way," Tommy explained. "So we're simply having a conversation with our family completely out of his way."

Horace's lips quirked and for a moment, Evelyn thought her father was going to laugh. However, he pulled his thin lips back into a flat line. "I'm not going to tell you anything different than I told him. Or anything more. Regardless of whether we are family or not."

"I'm actually very frightened, Father."

Evelyn hoped there was a softer part of her father living inside his rather austere outward persona and that he would think enough of her to do all that he could to help them catch the killer. Unless, of course, he was involved. She hadn't yet allowed herself to think too deeply about her father's possible participation in both the Carpelli scandal as well as the potential blackmail and the murder that occurred as a result, but she knew that she must to get to the bottom of what had happened.

"Whatever do you mean, Evelyn?" Martha frowned quizzically at her daughter.

"Mr Billingham was murdered, Mother, here on the grounds of this very estate. He had received a letter which we believe to be similar to the one Father received. I am very worried that the murderer will not stop until he is caught, and scared he may come after someone I love next."

"Horace?"

Evelyn tried not to let it bother her that her mother sought confirmation from her father on the authenticity of her explanation. She was a grown up, not a child any longer, and had spent three years during the war working for the police herself. Why was her word not enough?

"Evelyn is correct, Martha. I share her concerns."

"As you say, dear." Martha inclined her head, in complete agreement now that her husband had spoken.

Over the years, Evelyn had always presumed her father reminded his wife when to eat and when to sleep because she was always so busy with her dogs. Now she was beginning to believe that was simply her mother's personality—she needed to be told by her husband when to do certain things. Goodness only knew she had not been a very good mother, perhaps that was because there had rarely been anyone around to tell her what to do. Their father, as a member of parliament, had spent more time in London than he had with his family in east Yorkshire.

Evelyn was never more glad than right at the moment that she had a husband who not only allowed her to think for herself, but actively encouraged her to do so. On that occasion, it made more sense to allow Tommy to do the talking as it was obvious both of her parents were more willing to listen to him.

"Did Andrews keep the letter you brought to him last night?"

"Yes, he did." Horace took another puff on his cigar. "However, I can remember exactly what it said."

"Was the note hand or typewritten?" Tommy asked.

"Typewritten."

"And, to your knowledge, were all four notes exactly the same?"

"I didn't read my letter out when I was on the telephone, I merely asked each individual if they had received a letter referring to the Carpelli scandal."

"To clarify: you made telephone calls to Frederick Barrow, Sidney Payne and Robert Billingham? You spoke directly to each gentleman, and you did not speak to anyone else about the letter?"

"That is correct."

"And the wording of the letter?"

Horace blinked and drew heavily on his cigar. He paused for so long, Evelyn thought he was not going to answer. Eventually, he blew out smoke on a deep, heavy sigh. "I know what you did. I know that you prospered while my brothers suffered. Their blood stains your hands. The Carpelli scandal will not die as they did. If the price of my silence is not met, then Fleet Street shall know your shame. I will be in touch."

Evelyn shivered.

"Is that verbatim?"

"There may be the odd word that is different, but it is not paraphrased."

"That is clearly a blackmail letter." Tommy stared at his father in law through narrowed eyes. "You said yesterday that you had received a letter suggesting the press had new information regarding the scandal. That was inaccurate, at best."

"New information must have surfaced, so far as the writer believes, otherwise why would he write now after all this time? Why would he not have written and demanded money when the scandal first broke?"

"Is there any veracity to their statement?"

Horace met Tommy's gaze head on. This time he did not pause or seem to think about his answer before he spoke. "Not so far as I am concerned. Though I cannot speak for the others, that is why I invited them here this weekend. I wanted to clear my name once and for all."

"Why do you believe Billingham was killed?"

"The rogue who sent the letter must have murdered him."

Evelyn shook her head. "That makes absolutely no sense. If the writer of the letter wanted money from Mr. Billingham, why would they kill him?"

"Maybe Billingham paid and then the murderer killed him so he couldn't reveal who the blackmailer was?" Tommy mused.

"Or Billingham refused to pay and so was murdered," Evelyn added.

"The truth may be one of these scenarios," Tommy said. "But equally it may be something else entirely. However, it does seem clear that Billingham had been in contact with the person who wrote the letters and then, for an as yet undetermined reason, was killed. You must be very careful, sir."

"You believe I am in danger?"

"I believe you and your friends are all at very great risk of being approached by this villain and I would not wish you to fall prey to the same fate. If anyone should contact you—by letter, in person or over the telephone regarding this matter you must tell Detective Inspector Andrews at once."

"And you too, presumably?" Horace's lips quirked up in a half smile.

"I would be most grateful if you did." Tommy grimaced. "Despite my promise to the detective, I simply cannot sit idly by while people are threatened and murdered around me and my home."

"Very well," Horace agreed.

"You are my family and I take my responsibilities towards my family very seriously indeed," Tommy told him. "I give you my word that I shall not rest until I uncover the identity of this scoundrel."

***

Evelyn still felt very upset when she left the billiard room and went in search of Edith Billingham. She had not spoken to her guest alone since she and Tommy had found Robert's body. Not only did she want to see if there was anything Edith needed following the tragic turn her life had taken, but Evelyn also wanted to find out anything she could about Robert that may have led to his death.

Whilst she completely agreed with Tommy and believed the murder had occurred as a direct result of the blackmailing letters, she did not want to be pigeonholed into one way of thinking and therefore miss a clue or piece of information because she was too busy focussing on one aspect of the case.

After checking with the staff that Edith wasn't in her room, Evelyn checked all of the communal areas she could think of before eventually finding the new widow in the stables.

Nancy danced around her ankles, as she usually did when her mistress walked around the grounds of Hessleham Hall. Davey, however, was sleeping after a long walk into the village with Evelyn's maid, Doris, earlier that day.

"Mrs Billingham?"

Edith turned from where she had been standing, leaning into one of the stalls and rubbing the nose of a beautiful grey horse Evelyn should probably remember the name of. The dogs were her interest, horses were Tommy's.

"Lady Northmoor." Edith hadn't seemed a very effusive woman in the short time that Evelyn had made her acquaintance but her voice was completely flat and devoid of any emotion whatsoever.

"I do apologise for intruding upon your thoughts. I simply wanted to know if there was anything I could do to help you? I am aware Detective

Inspector Andrews has asked that everyone stay at the house and, as hostess, I am keen to make your stay with us as bearable as possible. Especially under the terrible circumstances."

"What could you possibly do to help me?" the other woman asked rudely.

"I really do not know," Evelyn said smoothly, ignoring Edith's bad manners. "But if you think of anything, I do hope you will let me know."

"I should like to take my meals in my room." Edith looked back toward the horse and away from Evelyn. "I do not care to be in the company of that awful woman Ann Payne."

"I believed you to be friends," Evelyn said conversationally.

"Our *husbands* were friends," Edith clarified. "Ann is a terrible flirt, especially for a woman of her advancing years and Margaret is an insufferable bore. And as for your mother…"

Evelyn nodded. "My mother is rather absent minded."

"That is putting it mildly," Edith replied curtly. "And much more polite than I would have been."

Evelyn didn't doubt it. It was clear that no one had told Edith that whilst honesty was indeed a very admirable trait, there really was no substitute for good manners. Particularly when discussing a family member—whilst you were staying in that person's home!

"If it would make you feel more comfortable, I would be glad to arrange for you to take meals in your room." Evelyn paused, she needed to choose her next words very carefully. "Is there anything more we can do on an evening for you? Perhaps we could arrange for you to have a glass of hot milk or some cocoa before you retire for the night? I understand you had trouble sleeping last night."

"Whatever gave you that idea?"

"You mentioned Mrs Payne was wandering the corridors. I presumed you must have found it difficult to sleep and that is how you saw her. Forgive me if I have misunderstood."

Edith stared at Evelyn shrewdly, she may well be rude and not care if her comments upset someone's feelings but Evelyn didn't think she would go so far as to call her a liar to her face. "I am not an old lady and I do not require a milky drink before bed."

"As you wish, Mrs Billingham."

"Let us not pretend we don't know what is going on, Lady Northmoor." Edith bent to pat Nancy on the head. "You are aware Mrs Payne monopolised my husband at dinner because you were forced to talk to that boring doctor all evening."

"Dr Mainwaring is a dear friend," Evelyn said, making a mental note that she had not talked to either Teddy nor Isolde after her brief matchmaking session with the doctor the evening before. "I don't find him at all boring."

Though, in actual fact, she had when she first met him. On the evening Tommy's uncle Charles had fallen ill earlier that summer, she had sat next to Teddy at dinner and had found it very difficult to engage him in intelligent conversation.

Memories of that dinner triggered another thought in Evelyn. How long had it been since she had written to Isobel Turnbull? And what was the name of the new vicar that was due to arrive in the next few weeks? She could remember Milly telling her, but the details had quite flown out of her mind.

Not for the first time since becoming Lady Northmoor, Evelyn thought that she might need a secretary to remind her of all the things she had to do, the people she needed to write to, the committee meetings she must attend and the people in the village she should visit. Perhaps if people didn't keep getting murdered around her, it would be easier to remember to do the more mundane, day to day things that seemed to slip her mind.

"It is very clear to me," Edith spoke slowly, as though she wanted to be certain Evelyn was taking notice of every word she said. "That Ann Payne was having an affair with my husband. You saw how Sidney jumped in last night to defend her. I expect he killed my poor Robert in a fit of jealous rage."

It was, of course, a reasonable hypothesis. Edith was right, she *had* noticed Ann whispering to Robert at dinner, their discussion seeming so private it excluded anyone else from having a conversation with either of them.

"That is certainly possible, Mrs Billingham." Evelyn wished she could see the reaction on Edith's face to her next question but the other woman was completely engrossed in stroking Nancy. "You do not believe that your husband's death had anything to do with those dreadful letters?"

"I do not." Edith looked at her then, spite flashing in her eyes. "My husband was cleared of any wrongdoing in the Carpelli scandal when he was alive. I will not have his name besmirched now he is dead."

Edith Billingham stalked off towards the house, moving remarkably quickly for a middle aged woman. As Evelyn had noticed earlier that day she did not seem as though she were grieving for her husband. Neither did Evelyn believe that she had told her all that she knew.

***

Tommy found Frederick Barrow later that afternoon trying to write a letter in the billiard room. The man didn't seem as though he was finding the missive particularly easy to write given the page was blank and he had spent more time filling his pipe with tobacco than with a pen in his hand.

"Do you mind if I join you?" Tommy indicated the paper. "I should hate to disturb you."

"Would be glad of the company, old chap, do sit down."

"Can I get you a drink?" Tommy looked at his watch. "The ladies will have finished afternoon tea."

Frederick Barrow smiled. "Then it seems quite acceptable for us to have a drink ourselves."

"I am certain my wife would think it a little early in the day," Tommy said conspiratorially. "Brandy?"

"Yes, please." Frederick tapped the side of his nose. "Best keep it our little secret then, I wouldn't want you to get into trouble with that charming wife of yours."

"She is rather, isn't she?" Tommy couldn't help but smile. He was every bit as in love with Evelyn as he had been the day he first saw her and he didn't care a jot that it wasn't really the done thing to admit those feelings to other people. "I am the luckiest man alive."

"Indeed you are." Frederick nodded, his expression downcast.

Tommy immediately felt contrite. It was a little thoughtless for him to be bragging about how marvellous his wife was when Frederick had married a quite peculiar woman who seemed to enjoy draping dead animals around her shoulders. He had heard the tale from Evelyn about how Davey had stolen it from one of the drawing room sofas and ran out into the garden with it firmly clamped between his teeth.

"I understand you have known Lady Northmoor's father for many years?"

"That is correct." Frederick's expression brightened. "Your wife may not recall, but I remember visiting Hessleham when she was a very young child. That was when Horace, Sidney, Robert and myself were all first friends."

"Were you all young MPs at the time?"

"No, not at all." Frederick smiled at what were clearly happy memories. "We knew each other slightly from school and started travelling in the same circles when we were in London. All northern boys together, you know?"

"Of course, it makes sense you would all become close with your shared backgrounds." Tommy almost wanted to just let Frederick talk, he didn't really need to ask the other man the questions he had planned to as it seemed he may receive the answers he sought if he simply listened. "Were you all in business back then?"

"That is correct." Frederick nodded. "We all started running, or at least were heavily involved in our family businesses back then. Robert was actually the first one of us to become interested in politics, yet he was the last one to become a member of parliament."

"I do hope you won't find this question impertinent." Tommy brought their drinks over and passed one to Frederick. "But if Robert was not a politician until recently, how was it that he became involved in the Carpelli scandal with the rest of you?"

"Robert worked as an business advisor to the War Office. The idea to use Carpelli Industries came from him to the minister in charge of procurements. Whether it was Robert, or another advisor, who recommended them to the minister I do not know."

"The equipment that Carpelli supplied was inadequate?"

"Not fit for bloody purpose!" Frederick said brusquely. "Men died because of its poor quality."

Tommy sucked down a sudden rush of burning anger. He had seen men be seriously injured, maimed, or even die because the equipment they had been supplied with by the British Army was not up to snuff. Whether or not it had come from Carpelli Industries, he did not know, and it didn't really matter. That particular company had sent out kit that had been damaging to soldiers, whether it was comrades Tommy knew or not.

He looked down at his hand, wrapped tightly around his glass of brandy. His knuckles were turning white. Tommy drew in a deep breath and slowly made himself relax.

"I say," Frederick said, leaning forward in his chair. "Are you alright, man?"

"Memories." Tommy put the glass on the table next to him and rubbed a hand across his face. "Sometimes weeks go by without me thinking of the war and other times the horror is constantly in my thoughts."

"This must be very difficult for you." Frederick finished his brandy. "There you were off fighting and meanwhile back at home, people like those who owned Carpelli were becoming rich on the back of the misery of soldiers."

The man's words struck a thought in Tommy's mind, something about the letter Horace had narrated to them and what Frederick had just said. Perhaps knowing who owned Carpelli Industries would give them the clue that they needed to work out who wrote the letters.

"Do you know who owned that particular company?"

"I do not." Frederick shook his head decisively. "I do hope, Lord Northmoor, that you do not think I had anything to do with that outrageous episode."

"Obviously I was away when the scandal broke," Tommy said. "But, as I understand it, you were completely exonerated."

"Yes, indeed." Frederick laughed then, a completely mirthless sound. "Perhaps if I had been involved, I would be a sight richer than I am now. I would imagine if I had received a share of the backhander, as was alleged, I would not now be attempting to write a letter to my wife's family to beg for a loan. Margaret has no idea, of course, but we are quite broke."

Tommy didn't know the salary of a member of parliament, but he thought it would be very reasonable—certainly more than he earned when he was in the police force. "I am desperately sorry to hear of your predicament."

"I can see that you are wondering how my affairs have reached such a dire state." Frederick looked longingly at his empty glass, as though he wished it would magically refill itself, but he already knew brandy was not the answer. "Sadly my family business failed during the war. I tried everything to save it, but I was not successful. Since then, Margaret has refused to listen to my pleas to curb her spending and she still makes purchases that are far beyond our means. I fear we have debts all over London that I have no way of repaying."

"There really is no way other than asking her family for help?"

"I have tried everything." For one awful moment, Tommy thought the other man was going to cry before he pulled himself together and shrugged. "I had better get on with it and just write the blasted letter."

As Tommy left Frederick to his missive, he couldn't help but wonder if the man had been lying to him about Carpelli. Was it possible when he said he had tried everything to raise money that one of the things he had attempted was blackmailing his friends?

Chapter Six

Evelyn had spent a long time trying to work out how best to approach Ann Payne. Should she simply repeat Edith Billingham's accusations and ask Ann if they were true? Should she try and find a way to ask the question without offending her? Or ought she to concentrate on trying to find out what Ann and Robert were talking about the night before he was killed?

Ann was in what the family called the music room. Evelyn didn't know how long it had been referred to by that name, but she had never known anyone in the Christie family to play music.

However, Ann was sitting on the piano stool running her fingers over the keys.

"Good afternoon, Mrs Payne." Evelyn inwardly grimaced. Her voice was too bright and sounded forced, even to her own ears.

"Oh, Lady Northmoor, do excuse me." Ann closed the lid of the piano.

"Mrs Payne," Evelyn said and relaxed into the conversation. This was not going to be as awful as talking to Edith Billingham had been. "It is I who should excuse myself. I feel as though I am intruding. Do you play?"

"I do." Ann nodded. "Though I would not be so presumptuous as to play in your home without permission."

"Oh goodness." Evelyn's mouth twisted in a wry smile. "Do you think Tommy and I so stuffy that you dare not play a piano without permission?"

"Not at all, Lady Northmoor." Ann shook her head to emphasise her words. "You have both been exceedingly accommodating and I am sure you know neither of you are in the least bit stuffy."

"Then you must agree, right now, to treat this house as if it were your own. Please feel free to play the piano, to read a book from the library, to ride a horse from the stable. You must not feel like you require an invitation to do any of those things."

"You are very kind," Ann said. "I should like to play the piano, if I may. I find it very relaxing."

"Perhaps, whilst I am here, you wouldn't mind talking to me about what happened to poor Mr Billingham?"

"What would you like to know?" Ann folded her hands in her lap as though she couldn't trust her hands not to touch the keys of the piano again.

"What were you talking about with him at dinner the evening before he died?"

"That's very abrupt, Lady Northmoor." Ann swiveled on the piano stool to stare out of the window that overlooked the perfectly manicured lawn. There wasn't a fallen leaf anywhere that Evelyn could see to mar the lush green surface.

"I could spend time skirting around what I really want to ask you but I can see you are keen to play so I thought I would simply come straight out and ask you what I would like to know."

"It was a private matter." There was a small but very secretive smile playing on Ann's lips that Evelyn did not like. It reminded her somewhat of her sister-in-law Lillian. Like a sly cat that had got the cream, as the old saying went. "However I can assure you that Robert and I were not having an affair, no matter what Edith says."

"I suppose that means that you will not tell me where you were going later that evening when Mrs Billingham saw you in the corridor?"

Ann shrugged. "You heard me say where I was going. I was searching for someone to ask for a drink of water. That is absolutely all there is to it."

"And if I was to ask you if you knew who had sent the letters your husband and his friends you received, you would tell me you know nothing?"

"It would be the truth." The smile had fallen from Ann's face, but something unpleasant lurked in the depths of her eyes. "They were exonerated. That is the limit of my knowledge of cash for contracts and the Carpelli scandal."

"What did you do for a living before you married Mr Payne?" Evelyn changed the track of their conversation abruptly.

"Why does that matter?"

"It doesn't." Evelyn shrugged. "I am simply curious. You're gazing at my piano as though you haven't seen one in years and you are positively longing to play it. I can see that. It makes me wonder why you do not have a piano in your home if you miss playing so very much."

"How do you know we don't have one?" Ann sneered.

"I don't," Evelyn said. "But you haven't, have you?"

"I worked in the music halls." Ann lifted her chin defiantly, as though admitting such a thing made her instantly more inferior socially. Which, of course, it did to much of society. "Though I wasn't an actress. I was in the chorus line. I danced."

"Music is very important to you."

Ann blew out a harsh breath and her shoulders relaxed a little. "It is, but Sidney is afraid if I have it in the house, I will want to go back there and give up the life that we have together."

"He has banned music from your home?" Evelyn couldn't prevent the total shock from sounding in her words. She knew she was lucky having a husband like Tommy but there were some days that could scarcely comprehend the lives some women lived with their spouses.

"It's because he loves me so very much." Ann lowered her voice. "He simply couldn't bear it if he thought he would lose me. So he buys me whatever I want whenever I want and I choose to give up music."

Sidney had been angry the evening before when Edith suggested Ann might be having an affair with Robert. At the time, Evelyn had believed it was simply chivalry on Sidney's part and he was defending his wife's honour. Now she couldn't help but wonder if there was something more sinister behind his reaction and whether that had led to him seeking Robert out early the next morning for a showdown.

"Do you think it is possible that your husband killed Robert in a jealous rage?"

"Oh I should think almost anything is possible," Ann said carelessly. "Sidney could have killed him, perhaps Edith killed him because she was sick and tired of his affairs, Frederick is stony broke so maybe he was blackmailing him."

"I suppose you're right."

"Of course I'm right. Blackmailing letters, money, jealousy. All are a perfect recipe for a murder."

There wasn't really anything Evelyn could say in response to that because what Ann said was correct. The main motives for the majority of murders was greed, sex or someone being in the wrong place at the wrong time.

"I believe your husband is out riding with Lord Northmoor so you will have some time to enjoy your music before he returns."

Ann smiled and for the first time since she arrived at Hessleham Hall, she looked truly happy. "Thank you. As I said earlier, you are very kind."

***

"After spending months in London, I am always shocked how beautiful it is out here." Sidney Payne stopped his horse on the bridle path at the top of a hill overlooking the North Sea.

"I find it difficult to cope with all the people in London," Tommy said in return. "The noise, the increased traffic, the pace of life. Things in the country are much more relaxed and quiet."

"Until someone gets murdered practically on your doorstep." Sidney looked over at Tommy.

"Yes, that has rather interfered with our quiet lives."

"I understand there has been a journalist poking around too."

"Really?" Tommy asked. "Where did you hear that?"

"Can't remember," Sidney said gruffly. "But I heard he is staying at the pub in the village and has been asking all manner of questions to everyone he meets."

This must be the young fellow Evelyn had told him about. He could remember her telling him that she had foisted him off to Aunt Em on the day of the fete. It may well be worth him asking his aunt what the man had wanted to know.

"My wife and her sister encountered him shortly after Billingham had been found dead. He claimed to be covering the fete for a York based newspaper but Evelyn found his story to be highly unlikely."

"Do you think he might have something to do with the letters?"

"Yes." Tommy nodded. "I think that may very well be possible. The letters, I believe, refer to someone in the press knowing about the scandal and here is a journalist apparently writing about a little village event. It does not add up to me."

"I can't think what that chap thinks he knows." Sidney stared out to sea. "There simply isn't anything for him to find, however many questions he asks."

Perhaps he had already found out what he wanted to know. He could have spoken to Billingham, received information, then killed him so he wouldn't be uncovered.

"Might Billingham have known something and paid the man to remain quiet?"

"Billingham wasn't really that sort." Sidney turned back to face Tommy. "I gather you did not know him well?"

"Not at all, actually," Tommy admitted. "He was my father in law's friend, as you know. It was he who asked me to invite you all here this weekend and as Billingham had been asked to open the fete, it seemed like a good idea."

"If Billingham had known anything about the arrangement Carpelli may have had with the government, he would not have paid someone to keep quiet about his involvement. He was a man who believed completely in his own infallibility. Had this fellow from the newspaper approached him, Billingham would have fronted it out."

"Perhaps he was killed because he *wouldn't* pay," Tommy mused.

"Robert was the only one out of the four of us who had the sort of money that a blackmailer would be satisfied with." Sidney kicked his horse into a walk. "While we all receive, or received in Horace's case, a decent wage and have a modest family income none of us are cash rich."

"Apart from Billingham?"

"It is an open secret in the city that Barrow is flat broke. Probably the only person that doesn't know, or pretends that they don't know, is his wife.

Horace and I are both second sons. Billingham didn't have family money on his own side, but I understand his wife's family are filthy rich."

The horses picked their way easily along the bridle path as the ground was still quite firm. Within weeks, Tommy was aware that this particular path was not one that would be safe for him to travel on horseback. The rain would come and leave the narrow track thick with mud. It was yet another thing that year that would change and, in Tommy's mind, not for the better.

Seasons had to come and go, that was as old as time, and he accepted that. Personally, however, his life was unrecognisable now in comparison to the first time he had ridden this way earlier that year.

Back then, he had been hopeful his leg would heal well enough for him to rejoin his role in the police force. He had lived with Evelyn in a sweet little cottage in the village and their life had been simple yet incredibly happy. Now they were Lord and Lady Northmoor with more demands on their time and energy than Tommy had ever thought possible. The responsibilities were enormous, but were not something that he could walk away from—he may well have his faults but one of them was not a lack of honour.

"I find myself quite unable to work out what is going on." Tommy said, a frustrated note in his voice. "It's infuriating, nothing seems to make sense or fit together."

"Best leave it to the police, old man," Sidney suggested, clearly unaware of Tommy's background.

"You're probably right," Tommy agreed though, of course, he had no intention of waiting for Detective Inspector Andrews to get to the bottom of the muddle of clues and misinformation that the case seemed to contain. "Is Billingham's wife usually so uncontrolled? She was jolly nasty to your wife last night."

"It must have been the shock." Sidney's jaw set tightly which clearly showed his displeasure at the turn of conversation, even though his voice did not betray his feelings. "She has always been similar in personality to Billingham. A little haughty, thinks herself above everyone else, but particularly Ann."

"Why particularly Ann?"

"Edith is aware that Ann once worked in music halls. Even though it was over thirty years ago, she has never let my wife—or me—forget it. There was nothing untoward about her employment, never a suggestion she did other sorts of…activity. Yet Edith would never accept Ann on the same social footing as herself. Even when Billingham and I became MPs, she would take every opportunity she could to show Ann up."

Tommy was able to easily fill in the gaps in Sidney's impassioned speech. Whilst Ann may have worked on the stage, that did not mean that she herself engaged in the type of immoral behaviour many others in that profession did with notoriety.

Robert Billingham, and his wife, were clearly not very pleasant people and even their 'friends' did not have anything particularly nice to say about them. With Robert Billingham dead, Tommy couldn't help but wonder if his wife might be next.

***

Evelyn found Isolde wrapped up against the cold, sitting outside on one of the wooden benches in the garden. "Can I sit with you?"

"I think I would rather we walk," Isolde replied looking as uncomfortable as her words. "If it is all the same to you?"

"Of course," Evelyn replied, looking at her new friend in concern.

The happy go lucky personality Evelyn had been so drawn to the first day she met Isolde had completely vanished. Left behind was a shadow. Even her vibrant hair seemed a darker red though that could just be the change in the weather. Rain was definitely on its way. The clouds were heavy, and the air felt damp and chilly.

"I suppose you are going to want to ask me about what happened at the fete?"

What *had* happened at the fete?

Evelyn stopped herself from asking the question. If she said the words out loud, Isolde was likely to make up a story in an attempt to satisfy Evelyn. No, she needed to find some other way of getting Isolde to tell her what had occurred.

"Only if you want to tell me." Evelyn crossed the fingers on her left hand behind her back. Being deliberately deceitful wasn't something that she enjoyed, especially towards someone that she liked.

"I had the most horrible feeling that I was being watched." Isolde shuddered at the memory. "You know when the hairs on the back of your neck prickle? Oh listen to me, I sound so melodramatic!"

"No, go on," Evelyn encouraged.

"My spine was tingling as though a thousand tiny little creatures were running up and down my backbone. It was frightfully annoying, but I simply could not shake that sensation off."

"And was there someone watching you?" Evelyn inspected Isolde's face carefully for any outward sign of emotion. Isolde stopped walking abruptly and looked behind her. "Do you feel someone watching you *now*?"

"I didn't until I mentioned it to you, but now I feel scared all over again."

"I expect it's because of the murder. It would be very odd if we weren't all a little frightened after what happened."

"No." Isolde shook her head emphatically. "It's not that. I do feel a little anxious because of that, but this is different."

"Are you able to explain?"

"What happened to that man was awful, but it wasn't personal to me. I know how jolly self absorbed that sounds. However, I didn't know him so although it was sudden and quite awful, it didn't concern me."

"But whoever was watching you at the fete was peculiar to you?"

"Oh Evelyn," Isolde sighed. "I should have simply come to talk to you last night. I knew you would understand. But I still felt so very silly because of what happened."

"We have not known each other very long at all," Evelyn said. "But I do hope that you know that you can trust me and you must talk to me about your worries. Whoever else would you tell?"

"That is just it, isn't it? I do feel that a girl should always have a friend she can confide in."

"Do you feel able to confide in me?" Evelyn asked. "Or, more properly, perhaps I should ask if you *want* to tell me what is troubling you? Feeling able to, wanting to, and actually doing it are all very different things."

"I feel able," Isolde confirmed. "In that I know I could trust you with my deepest darkest secret and you wouldn't tell a soul. I feel that about you. I *want* to tell you because it will unburden me. But I cannot."

Isolde breathed in tremulously as though she were trying desperately to hold in tears. Evelyn wanted to comfort her friend, but she also wanted to know what was worrying her so much. Isolde was definitely attempting to persuade Evelyn that the way she was feeling had nothing to do with the murder, but how could events not be linked? Prior to his death, Isolde was bright and vivacious and—Evelyn had believed—well on her way to falling in love with Teddy Mainwaring.

"If you cannot tell me what it is, I shall respect that. However you should know that I simply will not allow you to stay in my home and be concerned that someone is watching you. I will not have any guest of mine—any *friend* of mine—experiencing such troubling thoughts. Now what should we do to make you feel more comfortable?"

"I am so lucky to have met such a sweet friend." Isolde gave Evelyn a brief hug. "I do not know how I can feel more settled though. I do know that running away and almost upsetting poor Miss Armstrong's jam display was not the answer."

Now Evelyn knew what happened at the fete. It wasn't quite the remarkable event she had imagined given Isolde's reaction. Though almost knocking over a display wasn't the problem, it was whatever—or whoever—had elicited such a strong gut feeling in Isolde that her first response was to run away.

"We must make sure that you are not left alone so we can minimise your worries. If you want to come outside and I am busy or you cannot find me, speak to Doris and bring Nancy out with you. I am sure she will bring you comfort and perhaps make you feel a little more safe."

"Thank you, I shall do that. I do like being outdoors. I spend so many hours inside while I am preparing lessons, teaching, and then marking work that I don't like to be inside when I have free time."

"Absolutely understandable." Evelyn was pleased to see that Isolde now had some colour in her cheeks and her emotions seemed to be under control. "Now, about Dr Mainwaring. Has he been able to speak to you."

Isolde's hands flew up to cover her cheeks. "I was still so distressed last night at dinner that I am afraid I was rather rude to poor Dr Mainwaring."

"How so?"

"He worked extremely hard to engage me in conversation." Isolde smiled at the memory. "I think he had been practising and it was so very charming of him. The poor man must think I am incredibly unreliable and silly. I wanted to gain his attention, received it, and then he will think I have spurned him."

"I would be very happy to explain that your day had been troubling," Evelyn suggested. "If you would like me to. I would also think it likely he would enjoy a walk around the gardens with you. Perhaps his company would help to make you feel safe?"

"Perhaps it would."

"That is settled then. I shall let Dr Mainwaring know you were not quite yourself yesterday and suggest he asks you to take a walk before dinner."

"Quite the little matchmaker aren't you?" Isolde seemed to remember something as her expression turned serious once more. "Though one can never have enough friends, can one?"

"I rather thought you might both want a little more than a friendship?"

"Oh, Evelyn, I do! I truly do!"

"Then what is…"

Isolde let out a sob. "I feel so very ashamed. If you only knew what I was hiding you certainly wouldn't wish to still be my friend. Neither would you encourage your friend to romance me. Whatever am I to do?"

Despite Evelyn's repeated promises that it was quite safe for Isolde to share her worries, the tall redhead refused to say anything more on the matter. The entire exchange left Evelyn feeling even more confused than she had before they had begun their conversation.

Chapter Seven

As soon as Tommy returned from his ride with Sidney Payne, he telephoned down to the village to see if Ernest Franklin was still resident at the Dog & Duck Public House.

He was able to speak to George Hughes, the proprietor, who confirmed that Mr Franklin had not yet checked out. Tommy asked the pub landlord not to let his guest know he was coming to see him.

Usually Tommy would have walked the relatively short distance into the village but as it was not too long until dinner, he had asked Arthur Brown to bring the car round. When Tommy had stayed at Hessleham Hall that summer, prior to him becoming Lord Northmoor, Brown had doubled as second footman and Tommy's valet.

Tommy had found the temporary valet a very likable chap and had discovered he had a great interest in cars. Although he was occasionally needed to serve as a footman, his more usual role these days was to act as chauffeur for the family.

"Jolly decent of you to take me to the village. I know you must be exceptionally busy with the extra visitors in the house."

"It is my pleasure, My Lord," Arthur Brown answered. "And the car did need a run out, it's been standing still for a few days now."

They pulled up outside the Dog & Duck, and Tommy glanced quickly at the church clock at the end of the street. "I shall be as quick as I can, Brown, then we can get back in time for us both to change for dinner."

Tommy jumped out of the car and hurried towards the old country pub. He knew George Hughes from the infrequent times he had stopped for a pint in the hostelry on his way home from work when he lived in the village.

"Long time no see!" the landlord greeted Tommy as he walked through the door. "My Lord, is it now?"

"That's right, George." Tommy grimaced. He was still very uncomfortable hearing himself referred to that way.

It seemed acceptable to him for old men, such as his Uncle Charles, who blustered their way through life accepting titles as their birthrights and the deference that went with them. Sadly, there had needed to be a good deal of family deaths via the war, the Spanish flu and finally cold blooded murder before the title had landed in Tommy's hands.

Tommy longed for George to refer to him as 'Christie' as he had back in the early summer when he had last visited the pub for a drink. However the rules of succession and etiquette had been in place long before he was born. His years of duty and service in the police force, and latterly the army, meant that although he may not understand why things were the way that they were, he did at least respect the traditions that had lasted many hundreds of years.

"I've kept a quiet table free in the corner so you can have a word with young Franklin. Not been bothering those guests you've got up at the manor, has he? He seems a nice enough fella."

"Not at all, George." Tommy smiled. "I just need to ask him a few questions about what he might have seen the afternoon of the fete."

"It was a bad business, that." George shook his head. "Not that he was a nice man, but no one deserves to die face down in a stream with a bloody great knife sticking in their back do they?"

"Indeed, George, couldn't have said it better myself."

When the landlord realised he wasn't going to get anything else out of Tommy about the murder, the circumstances, or the MPs character he reluctantly headed through a door marked 'private'.

Shortly afterwards he returned with Ernest Franklin who joined Tommy in the area George had indicated he'd reserved for them. Tommy watched the young man thoroughly scan the pub as he made his way over to the corner table.

"You wanted to see me?"

"Yes, Mr Franklin is it? We haven't met. I'm Tommy Christie." Tommy put out a hand, accepted by the young man who eyed him warily.

Ordinarily Tommy would never introduce himself as 'Tommy Christie', but this man—more of a boy, really—already looked terrified. Tommy wanted him to feel comfortable talking to him and he wouldn't if he was more concerned about getting his terms of address right than simply answering the questions Tommy put to him.

"Ernest Franklin. Pleased to meet your acquaintance, I'm sure."

"You're visiting us from York, I understand?"

George arrived at the table then and unceremoniously plonked two tankards of beer on the table between Tommy and Ernest.

"Thank you, George. I'll settle up with you, later."

"That's right, yes. I'm from York. Here to cover the fete for my newspaper the York Times."

"The fete?" Tommy raised his eyebrows in mock surprise. "I wouldn't have thought that covered much space in such a large newspaper."

"Ladies like to read about that type of thing."

"Do they really?"

Ernest looked down at his beer though he made no move to pick it up and take a drink. He seemed to be waiting for Tommy to say more. When he realised it was definitely his turn to talk, he seemed lost for something to say. "Old ladies, mostly."

"Ah, like my Aunt Emily who I believe you spoke to during the fete?"

"Yes," Ernest muttered. "Lovely lady. Chattered on for hours about how things used to be done back in her day."

Tommy couldn't imagine that Aunt Em had ever 'chattered on' in her life. Let alone for hours and with someone like Ernest. He seemed a very average fellow and so was certainly not the type of man who would have been able to hold Em's attention for long.

"Have you finished writing your article?"

The question caught Ernest completely off guard. "Finished it? I…what do you mean?"

"Finished the piece on the fete," Tommy prompted. "And turned the finished article in to your editor, or whatever it is you newspaper journalists do."

George had not let lit the enormous fire to the left of where they were sitting and so there was no reason for Ernest to suddenly start sweating. Tommy could actually see beads of moisture sitting on the young man's forehead. Despite the very obvious fact that the youth was lying to him, Tommy couldn't help but feel a little sorry for him.

"Ah yes. That is, it's nearly finished."

"It must be very long," Tommy pressed. "Some three or four thousand words?"

"Somewhere around that long." Ernest agreed eagerly.

"And you write that all out in longhand, do you?"

"Longhand." Ernest nodded vigorously. "Yes, that's it. In longhand."

Now Tommy definitely felt sorry for the lad though it was tinged with a touch of anger. "Definitely no shorthand?"

"Sometimes there may be a bit of shorthand," Ernest seemed to recover himself. "If the need arises."

Tommy sat back in his chair and folded his arms. "It just seems a little odd to me that you are still here more than twenty four hours after the fete ended. No one at the fete saw you with a notebook, you don't seem to know your shorthand from your longhand. You clearly have no clue how long an article should be. And, moreover, the York Times has never heard of you."

"I…" Ernest opened his mouth as though to deny what Tommy had said, but wisely he closed it again.

Tommy had slipped into his old role as a detective as if he had never been away for a minute. The estate kept him busy and he had to admit he liked being able to ride whenever he wanted and learn more about the land he now owned. Up until that moment, however, he hadn't realised how much he enjoyed getting to the bottom of a witness' story and he felt he was now very close to getting information out of Ernest.

"Yes?" Tommy leaned forward, resting his elbows on the table in-between them.

Ernest pulled the mustard yellow handkerchief out of his breast pocket and used it to mop his forehead. "It's possible I haven't been entirely honest about why I'm here."

"Really?" Tommy drew out the word. "Perhaps you would like to let me know exactly why you are here in Hessleham?"

Ernest's eyes flashed with an emotion Tommy couldn't name and then instead of looking like a slightly pathetic boy, his face twisted into a mask of pain and sorrow. "The Carpelli scandal."

"You wrote the letters?" Tommy asked in a soft voice.

"I don't know what you mean."

"Oh do come on, the game is up."

Ernest roughly pushed back the chair he had been sitting on away from the table. "I don't have to talk to you. You might be lord of the manor, but you can't make me talk to you!"

Tommy wanted to bang his fist on the table in frustration, but he restrained himself. He had been so close!

"Locked himself in his room," George muttered.

Tommy asked George for a pen and paper and wrote a swift note to Ernest. "Please put that under his door."

"Of course, My Lord."

"And George?" Tommy paused as the landlord turned back to face him. He wasn't sure if saying more was the right or wrong thing to do. "Make sure you lock up well tonight and please keep an eye out for anyone suspicious prowling around."

"You think he murdered Billingham?" George jerked a thumb towards the upper floor of the room where the guests bedrooms were situated.

"I don't know if I think he committed the murder or whether he's in grave danger. I wish I had a better answer for you, George."

"No matter, My Lord. No one will be coming past me." George Hughes crossed his burly arms across his chest. "You can rely on me."

***

Meanwhile Evelyn had caught up with Margaret Barrow before she went upstairs to change for dinner. Not wanting them to be disturbed, she had drawn the older lady into the music room. Some of the men were already occupying the billiard room and, of course, the police were still ensconced in the library.

"I wanted to check how you were, Mrs Barrow?" Evelyn inquired. "After the row last night and the terrible incident that has befallen Mr Billingham."

Margaret Barrow looked quite unmoved. These friends of her father's had certainly lived through some difficult years, but not one of them seemed to have any emotions. Or, at least, not any that they allowed others to see.

"I was a little perturbed when I couldn't find my stole the other day." Margaret looked accusingly at Evelyn. "But then it appeared under one of the cushions in the drawing room. After I had already searched there."

"I would imagine it was moved by someone in error and then replaced," Evelyn hated how easy it sometimes was to tell an untruth. Though, technically, Davey had made a mistake in taking the stole and 'someone' had definitely put it back. Evelyn consoled herself that she hadn't told an outright lie.

"I would imagine so." Margaret did not break eye contact with Evelyn. "I would hate for any of my things to go missing. They are so very expensive."

"Of course, Mrs Barrow." Evelyn reassured her. "I will speak to my staff and ensure that they take the utmost care over your things."

"Was there anything else, Lady Northmoor?" Margaret asked grandly.

"Well yes, as a matter of fact." Evelyn sat on the love seat near the window. She indicated a chair opposite. "Won't you please sit down?"

"I'd rather not." Margaret looked at the closed door. "We need to change for dinner."

"What can you tell me about the Carpelli scandal, Mrs Barrow?"

"Nothing at all!" Margaret flustered. "Why would you ask me such a thing?"

"You're aware your husband and his friends all received a particularly nasty letter?"

"Of course," she composed herself a little. "My husband tells me everything."

"Perhaps, then, he may have shared with you whether he intended to make contact with the blackmailer and offer him money?"

"How dare you?" Margaret said in a shrill voice. "You are implying that my husband knew the circumstances of the scandal. Only someone who knew whether money changed hands in exchange for a government contract would wish to pay the blackmailer for his silence."

"I beg your pardon," Evelyn said. "I certainly did not mean to offend you. I apologise unreservedly if I have caused you any offence. That certainly was not my intention."

Margaret swayed on her feet and caught hold of the door knob to steady herself. Evelyn rushed to the other woman's side.

"Take your hands off me, young woman!"

Evelyn backed away and watched as Margaret Barrow threw open the door and burst into the corridor as though she were being chased by a thousand madmen.

Of course, that would be the very moment that Detective Inspector Andrews walked out of the library. "Lady Northmoor?"

"I apologise if the noise disturbed you," Evelyn said. "Unfortunately Mrs Barrow lost her stole over the weekend and she's still rather upset about it."

Andrews looked towards the stairs to check Margaret Barrow was out of earshot. "I saw that ghastly thing only yesterday."

"Indeed." Evelyn nodded. "However, today she believes that someone took it out of her possession by way of a nasty joke. She did not take it very well."

"Indeed." The inspector echoed Evelyn. "I should hate to think you have been attempting to question your guests, Lady Northmoor."

"I assure you, that is most definitely not the case." Evelyn shook her head in what she hoped looked like genuine dismay. "I would never attempt to do such a thing against your strict orders."

"Lady Northmoor!" Doris exclaimed in a loud voice. "There you are! My goodness, I have been searching everywhere for you. Do excuse us, Detective Inspector, but I must get Lady Northmoor dressed for dinner otherwise she will be embarrassingly late."

He nodded and Evelyn following Doris to the stairs. As soon as they reached the sanctuary of her room, she held her head in her hands. "I have told so many half truths and complete stretches of the truth in the last few days, Doris, I don't know whether I am coming or going."

"Oh Lady Northmoor!" Doris laughed. "You've been spending too much time with young Nora coming out with such things."

"I suppose I should say I'm quite befuddled or such like?" Evelyn shook her head. "I didn't realise remembering to talk like a countess would be such hard work."

"Well, My Lady," Doris said. "I think you're doing a grand job. Now let us get you ready for dinner so you can carry that on."

***

After dinner, Tommy excused himself and met Evelyn and Aunt Em in the small room at the front of the house that he had appropriated for his own use earlier that summer. It had been the former smoking room of the grand old house and suited Tommy's purposes perfectly.

"Why must we hide in this poky old room?" Aunt Em asked as Tommy ushered them inside.

Tommy waited until his aunt had a chance to look around her. "You were saying, Aunt Em?"

"My apologies." She inclined her head. "You have performed quite the transformation."

The heavy velvet curtains that had kept out the natural light, but kept in the stale smell of years of tobacco were gone. Tommy had kept the large desk in the corner and hadn't taken down the dark panelling on the lower half of the walls. However, a fresh coat of white paint on the upper portion of the walls, proper light fittings, and a colourful rug in the middle of the room made it look entirely different.

"Evelyn and I wanted to talk to you, Aunt Em," Tommy said. "We must be quick as our guests will think we are exceedingly rude."

"I presume you have both been busy sleuthing your way around our guests?"

"Of course," Tommy said. "We couldn't just leave things as they are."

"Absolutely not," his aunt agreed. "As I said before that detective arrived, you are far more capable than he in apprehending the killer."

"We thank you for your faith, Aunt Em." Tommy smiled, though a little grimly. "I hope that it is not misplaced."

"How can I help?"

"We were wondering what you spoke to the reporter, Ernest Franklin, about at the fete. He suggested to Tommy that you had spoken for a long time."

"He asked me a few questions about Hessleham. Then asked if I knew Robert Billingham. I told him that was none of his business."

Evelyn laughed, she could just imagine the look she gave the young man while she told him off and put him in his place. "Then what did he ask?"

"He asked who the beautiful woman on the 'guess the weight of the cake' stall was."

"Did you tell him her name?" Evelyn's breath caught in her throat. She hadn't wanted to believe that Isolde was involved in this frightful mess, but she certainly seemed to be right in the middle of it.

"I told him I thought she was the schoolteacher from the village but I didn't know anything about her or where she was from." Aunt Em raised an eyebrow. "That was the right thing to do, was it not?"

Tommy nodded. "Yes, Aunt Em, it was. Well done."

"Of course by this point, I could tell that he wanted to get off because he wasn't getting any information from me."

"So what did you do next?" Evelyn asked, looking forward to the answer.

"I talked to him, at length, about every single villager I could see. I told him about Miss Armstrong and how the recipe for blackcurrant jam has been in their family for years. I mentioned how her brother, Percy, runs the post office."

"Oh, Aunt Em!" Tommy laughed out loud. "That poor man."

"I believe I was the poor one," Aunt Em said in her most majestic voice. "That man tried to catch me out with lies. I was not about to fall for it. My throat was quite parched by the time I had finished boring him to death."

Evelyn held her sides as she laughed. "You are quite magnificent. Whatever would we do without you."

"Let us hope you do not have to find out for a great many years yet." Em tapped her hand on the armrest of her chair. "Now, what else must you work out before you unveil the murderer?"

"I think we need to know who owns Carpelli Industries Limited," Tommy said. "I believe when we know that, we may have a vital clue in working out who the target of the blackmail was. Ernest definitely thought that one of the four friends knew something."

"He did not admit to sending the letters though, did he?" Evelyn clarified.

"No, he did not," Tommy admitted. "Though I am quite certain that he did. I think he meant for the letters to flush out the person he thinks is to blame. Though I'm still not completely convinced the cash for contract scenario is correct."

"But we do think that is what *Ernest* believes happened?"

"Without a shadow of a doubt." Tommy nodded. "I understand there is a place in London that holds records of every company that has been incorporated."

"We should send Florence to find that out." Florence was one of Charles's daughters. "It will give her something to do. I am certain that she would help us. I will telephone her in the morning."

"Marvellous." Tommy clapped his hands together. "Now, darling, what else do you think we need to find out?"

Evelyn didn't want to say the next words, but she knew that she must. "We have to find someone in York who knows Isolde. There is something she is hiding. Of that, I have no doubt. I do hope it isn't linked to this dastardly business, but I have learned not to believe in coincidences."

"Do we have family in York, Aunt Em, who can find that out for us?"

"We do, but I believe cousin Florence in London will be the best person to obtain that information. I will tell her she must visit Somerset House. That is where the records of all births, marriages and deaths are kept. There surely cannot be very many girls born in the York area named Isolde Newley."

Tommy looked at his wife. "Do you think that will help?"

"I think it will prove something rather than help as such."

"Whatever do you mean?"

"May I?" Aunt Em interjected. Evelyn motioned for her to carry on. "I would suggest that Evelyn believes there will be no record of an Isolde Newley born in the York area in the correct time frame. Am I right, dear?"

"Yes, Aunt Em, you are." Evelyn nodded. "I don't think she is who she says she is."

"Would there not be some record of who she really is with whoever employed her?" Tommy wondered. "Who does employ village school teachers?"

"I believe it is something to do with the church. Not the vicar, but maybe the church council. I shall go into the village tomorrow and find out."

"Now before we go rejoin the others," Tommy said. "I simply must know why you asked Ann Payne about her background?"

"I'm certain Aunt Em has some ideas about that, too?"

"She takes very good care of herself," Aunt Em remarked. "Extremely good care. One usually finds ladies who look so very put together are clever with make up and such like. Of course, anyone who works on the stage learns how to do that to their best advantage."

"That is what I thought. It was also how very scathing Edith was towards her. As though there was something hidden that everyone knew but never spoke about. Finally it was the way she looked at the piano." Evelyn shook her head sadly. "It was with a great sadness, like how a lady might look at a man she has loved and lost."

"She is a woman with a suppressed passion inside her." Aunt Em put a hand on Evelyn's arm. "Please be very careful, dear. If she has been denied this substantial love for many years there will be no limits to her frustration."

"I promise I shall be especially vigilant. There are a number of people around us with emotions I feel are dangerously volatile."

Tommy stood up and held his hands out to his wife. As he helped her to her feet, he softly pressed his lips to hers. "We must find out who is responsible quickly because I have a strong sense that there will be another victim very soon if we do not."

Chapter Eight

Early the following morning, Tommy went to see Dr Mainwaring before breakfast. Teddy had finished dressing and was sitting at the desk in his room. At Tommy's knock and shouted greeting, Teddy called out for him to enter.

"Good morning," Tommy said. "Busy day ahead?"

"I have a few house calls to make but Andrews has made it clear he wants me back here this evening."

"It seems a little silly that you're able to carry on your usual day to day activities but you have to return here after work." Tommy looked out of the window and, off in the distance, could see the spot next to the river where he and Evelyn had found the body of Robert Billingham. "Does the detective believe murders only happen after working hours?"

"Absolutely." Teddy chuckled. "I could easily visit old Mrs Harris, say I'd travelled the scenic route back to village and have plenty of time to come back here and bump someone off before going on to the pub to see Mrs Hughes."

"I kind of wish I thought that's what happened," Tommy said. "That someone came up from the village to commit the murder, I mean, then went home again. It's a little unsettling to think we are very probably sharing our home with the murderer."

I suppose that is what you have come to talk to me about? Not my silly little ramblings about driving around the country killing people. I hope you do not suspect me."

"Of course not, old man. I know you well enough by now to be certain you like to cure people and not kill them off. Besides which, you have no motive to kill Billingham."

"Ah, the old means, motive, and opportunity."

"That is correct. Almost everyone had the means and the opportunity." Tommy couldn't help but go through things out loud one more time. "You are aware that the murder weapon was a knife from our own kitchen?"

"Yes, the local bobby had me go down to the stream and certify death before Detective Inspector Andrews was sent for. He wanted to be certain Billingham was 'completely dead' before telephoning York."

"Goodness!" Tommy exclaimed, disbelievingly. "As opposed to 'sort of dead' or 'almost dead'. I should have said it was perfectly obvious looking at a distance no one could have survived that injury."

"It was a very large knife." Teddy nodded. "And even if by some miracle the stab wound had not penetrating any major organs, he fell face down in the stream, he wouldn't have lasted long in that position."

"Has a time of death been established, do you know?"

"They are not certain because the body was in the water but, taking into account the ambient weather, etcetera etcetera, the word is they are looking at within a couple of hours of him being found."

"That is consistent with what we have learned so far. It seems a very brazen attack to me," Tommy mused. "Although a person couldn't be identified from the house if they were down by the stream, they would certainly be recognisable as they returned."

"And it wasn't so early that there was no one about," Teddy added. "I suppose whoever it was is either lucky, mad, or very desperate."

"Probably all three." Tommy patted Teddy on the shoulder. "Now, about Miss Newley."

"Ah," Teddy replied. "I rather thought you would get around to that subject."

"How did things go at dinner?"

Teddy shrugged. "I am afraid it did not matter what I did or what I said, she simply was not interested. I am certain Evelyn must have misunderstood Miss Newley's interest in me. She couldn't have been more clear other than flat out telling me to shut up."

"I don't suppose…" Tommy began awkwardly.

"That I managed to find anything out?" Teddy finished with a wry twist of his lips. "Nothing. She gave monosyllabic answers to everything I asked. I tried enquiring as to where she studied to become a teacher and she stared at me as though she hadn't heard a word I said. It was most peculiar."

"Evelyn is going down to the village this morning to talk to the substitute vicar. She thinks the church council employed Miss Newley so surely they will know more about her and have seen her credentials and such."

"You must suspect her if you are investigating her?" Teddy asked with a note of sadness in his voice.

"We must look into everyone thoroughly. I know you understand that."

"Do you think Andrews will be following the same lines of enquiry as you?"

"He spends rather a lot of time on the telephone. I imagine he is getting officers at headquarters to look into things but I prefer to be actively pursuing rather than sitting back and waiting for answers. Though Aunt Em is asking cousin Florence in London to do some digging for us."

"Florence is Eddie's sister?"

"Correct." Tommy nodded. "She is the youngest of Eddie's six sisters and Aunt Em believes she can be trusted to be discreet and pass on what she knows without tittle tattling all over town. It won't do for the murderer to be tipped off that we are asking certain questions."

"I shall not compromise things by asking more," Teddy said, rising from the chair and moving over to the mirror to put on his tie.

"I do wish you would let me send someone to help you in a morning."

"Goodness gracious, Tommy." Teddy looked at his friend with undisguised horror. "I couldn't think of anything worse. I have been dressing myself in a morning for a good many years now and can manage perfectly well by myself. Anyway, I would imagine your staff are kept busy tending to the needs of the other gentlemen staying in the house."

"Indeed." Tommy nodded vigorously as a thought formed in his mind. "I perhaps need to speak to them, see if they have seen anything untoward. Whoever went down to the stream to attack Billingham must have worn a long overcoat or something similar in order to hide the knife in case they were seen."

"That's true." Teddy agreed. "Although we just agreed it was a brazen act, they surely would not have been so foolhardy as to walk through the grounds carrying a kitchen knife."

"I shall add talking to the staff to my list of things to do." Tommy walked towards the door. "But first, we must eat, I am positively famished."

Teddy chuckled. "I have never known you be anything but, my friend!"

***

Immediately after breakfast, Evelyn set off towards the village. She had written a letter she intended to deliver herself to the butcher stating how pleased she and Tommy were with the service provided to the house by Albert.

Accompanying her on the walk was Davey who barked at everything he saw and heard. Whilst neither Evelyn nor Tommy thought she was at any risk, she had agreed to take a whistle with her. Quite how much use that would be if a knife wielding madman accosted her on the lane to the village, Evelyn did not know. However, the noise the puppy made as he gambolled along sniffing at every single blade of grass and bush as he went would hopefully at least provide her with an early warning system.

She encountered no one on her short walk and with her errand at the butcher's complete, headed towards the vicarage. The previous vicar had moved away after only a very short stay in Hessleham and the current priest was temporarily looking after the parish until the permanent placement arrived.

Evelyn was hopeful that the man would be able to assist her in finding out how Isolde had been employed at the village school. To her regret, she realised that she had not attended church since before Oliver Turnbull left which was several months ago. Therefore she had never met the man who led worship at St Augustus.

"Good morning," she said brightly to the elderly man who opened the vicarage door to her. "I am Lady Northmoor and exceedingly pleased to meet you."

"Lady Northmoor!" the man exclaimed and held a hand to his chest.

Evelyn felt very uncomfortable. She hated it when people acted as though she was visiting royalty when they met her. In her mind, she was still plain old Evelyn Hamilton who had lived in the village her entire life.

"I do apologise," Evelyn said. "I have brought my puppy out for a walk and only now realised that you may not like dogs in the vicarage. Perhaps we could go for a walk? I would very much appreciate you answering some questions for me."

"Lady Northmoor, I should be pleased if you and your little friend will come through to the parlour with me. I shall ring for tea. Or is it coffee at this time?" He looked concerned, as though offering Evelyn the wrong beverage would somehow land him in trouble.

"I would be happy with whichever you are having."

Evelyn followed the man into a dark corridor. He leaned heavily on a cane as he walked, pushing open a door with his spare hand, he led the way into a small but neat parlour.

"Do sit down, Lady Northmoor." He moved over to the fireplace and pulled the long, thick cord that hung there.

"Vicar?" A voice sounded from the door immediately. "What can I get for you."

"Coffee, please, Elsie. For Lady Northmoor and myself."

"Of course, sir, I shall bring it through immediately."

"You must excuse the manners of an old man." The vicar's eyes smiled brightly at her through the wrinkles of his weathered face. "I am John Capes, vicar of this parish."

Evelyn returned his smile, he was a quite delightful man. She wished she had met him sooner as she had a feeling his sermons would be of the friendly sort, full of useful advice rather than the fire and brimstone type she remembered from her childhood.

"It seems we must both apologise for lapses in our behaviour," Evelyn said. "It has been too long since I have attended church. My sister, however, attends each week with her children. She has told me the name of the new vicar who is coming to Hessleham, but I regret that I cannot remember his name."

"Who is your sister?"

"Millicent Wilder. Her husband, Reg, is a doctor so isn't able to attend with her regularly."

"She is a very admirable young woman. Volunteers for lots of committees. Excellent at arranging things."

"Yes, that's Milly. She is remarkable."

"And you, Lady Northmoor, what do you do?"

"I suppose I do similar works to my sister, though on a much smaller scale." Evelyn looked down, pleased to see that Davey had curled up on the rug next to her chair and was fast asleep. "I have only recently come by my title and am not yet accustomed to the work that goes with it though I am trying very hard."

"I'm sure." He nodded kindly. "Though as Mrs Wilder's sister, I have every confidence that you will grow into your new position and manage your responsibilities every bit as admirably as she does."

"You are very kind."

Elsie returned then with a tray and the vicar poured coffee for them both. He handed her cup to her. "You must tell me the reason for your visit. You said you had some questions you wished me to answer."

"I am afraid they are of a rather sensitive nature so it may be that you will not wish to furnish me with answers."

"Ask the questions, Lady Northmoor, and I will see what I can do to the very best of my abilities."

"They are concerning the village schoolteacher, Miss Newley."

He blinked rapidly as soon as Evelyn mentioned Isolde's name. "Goodness, right. Lovely young woman."

"She is, isn't she?" Evelyn leaned forward slightly in her chair. "And that is the thing, Vicar, I like her very much but I am extremely afraid that she is not at all who she says she is."

"Would it relieve you if I were able to confirm that she is exactly who she says she is?"

"Yes, it would." Evelyn paused.

"But you need me to tell you how I know that?"

"I do really, yes."

"Perhaps if you tell me why you need this information, I can tell you as much as I am able without breaking a confidence?"

"Do you mean like a confession?"

"No, my dear, not a confession. Miss Newley has sins, like all of God's children, but she has nothing for which she needs to confess for. However, I am aware of personal information that I will not share. At least, not without her express permission."

Evelyn nodded. "I see. That is understandable. Now, Vicar, I must tell you that during the war I worked in the police force. My husband, prior to joining up and serving his country during the war, was also employed in that profession. Although we are no longer employed, we both retain an interest in solving crime."

"Are you telling me, Lady Northmoor, that you are investigating the murder of Robert Billingham?"

"Yes, Vicar, does that shock you?"

"I am seventy four years old. I have lost my capacity to be shocked."

Evelyn laughed. "I realise that it is extremely unconventional, but we have rather found that people prefer to tell us things that they wouldn't tell the police."

"I have not had the pleasure of meeting your husband, but I can certainly understand people telling you whatever you want to know." The vicar nodded to himself. "Mrs Wilder has that very same air you have of complete capability that gives people a reason to trust that she can be relied upon."

"I am pleased you think so. I admire my sister very much, so to be compared to her is a great compliment."

"Now we must get back on topic." The vicar tapped his cane gently on the floor. "You are investigating a murder and for reasons I shall not ask, you wish to know more about Miss Newley and if she is in fact the person that she claims to be."

"I thought because you had employed her, you would be aware of her suitability to teach school and possibly know more about her background."

"Yes, it is unusual these days for a church to still be in charge of employing schoolteachers. Nowadays it is usually governed by local Education Authorities. However, Hessleham is a relatively small parish and the school building is in excellent state of repair so the local authorities have no need to interfere. Whether that is a good or a bad thing is up for debate, of course."

Evelyn nodded her understanding. "Do go on."

"I have known Miss Newley for many years. In fact, I am the reason she came here. I was aware of the vacancy at the school after the previous teacher married and I recommended the post to her."

"So her name is Isolde Newley?"

"That is correct."

Evelyn finished her coffee. "I must say, I am very relieved."

"You like Miss Newley?"

"I do." Evelyn confirmed. "Very much. Which is why I am so pleased that she is not hiding who she is."

The vicar's expression fell for a moment before he brightened and smiled at her. He gestured to Davey. "What a good little fellow."

"Oh do not be deceived, Vicar, he is quite a naughty little chap when he wants to be." Evelyn stood up and Davey immediately got to his feet and stretched. "You have been very hospitable, but I must not take up any more of your time."

"One last thing, Lady Northmoor?" The vicar patted Davey's head. "If I were to tell you that I intend to stay in this parish, may we see you in church?"

"Yes, Vicar, I do believe that you will."

"What wonderful news." The vicar took his time standing and saw Evelyn to the door. "Do bring your husband with you. I am sure he has some interesting stories I would love to hear."

"Of course, Vicar, and thank you."

Evelyn was going to have some strong words with her sister. Why on earth hadn't Milly told her what a delightful man John Capes was?

Happy in the knowledge that, despite how oddly Isolde Newley was acting, it wasn't because she was hiding something sinister Evelyn walked back towards the lane that led to Hessleham Hall.

She had just reached the edge of the village when a woman ran from the Dog & Duck screaming. "Murder! Murder!"

***

"Mrs Hughes?" Evelyn reached the woman's side in seconds. "What on earth is the matter?"

"Didn't you hear me?" The woman shouted, panic in her eyes. "Murder in my pub. Murder, I tell you!"

"Whatever do you mean, Mrs Hughes?"

"I don't know how much plainer I can say it, Lady Northmoor." Annie Hughes burst into noisy tears. "He's dead in his room."

"Mr Hughes?"

"No." Mrs Hughes shook her head. "That young man your husband came to talk to last night. Dead."

"Are you absolutely certain?"

Annie Hughes sniffled. "I haven't touched him if that's what you mean."

"Here." Evelyn held out Davey's lead. "Hold my dog and I shall go check."

"But Lady Northmoor…"

Evelyn strode towards the pub. She went in through the front door and towards a plain door near the bar. A sound behind her startled her and she whirled around. She put a hand on her chest, willing her heart to stop beating quite so hard. "Mr Hughes, you scared me."

"I found him," the landlord said.

"Your wife said he is dead?"

"In his room."

"Does it look as though he may have died in his sleep?"

George Hughes looked at Evelyn as though she was mad. "With half his head smashed in?"

"Ah, I see." Evelyn peered at the man who sat in a dark corner of his pub. "You look rather like you could do with a brandy."

"Yes." He nodded at her and then held out his hands to her. They were shaking uncontrollably.

Evelyn had never seen anyone's hands tremble so violently in her life.

"May I get it for you?"

He nodded and Evelyn went behind the bar and returned with a glass of brandy filled slightly past the two fingers she knew Tommy usually poured for himself.

"Thank you, My Lady." George wrapped both hands around the glass and eased it slowly to his mouth.

"Mr Hughes," Evelyn said, casting a glance towards the door. "I wonder. Would it be alright with you if I checked to be certain that Mr Franklin is indeed deceased?"

"That's no sight for a woman." George shook his head. "My Annie about fainted cold when she saw him."

"I understand it's a frightful sight." Evelyn nodded. "But I would like to check."

"Up them stairs." George gestured towards a door next to the bar. "Second door on the left."

Evelyn moved away from the terrified man and towards the door he had indicated. "Will you be alright if I leave you. Just for a moment?"

George looked at his hands which were still shaking and a look of shame passed across his face. "It's the war, Lady Northmoor, I still have nightmares. And seeing that young fellow and the blood…it brought it all back. It's no sight for a lady."

Evelyn nodded. There was nothing she could do to make this man feel better and as the wife of a returned soldier, she was aware of the horrors these men still carried round with them. His embarrassment that she had seen him this way surrounded him like a shroud.

"I will be just a moment."

She opened the door and went up the stairs. Halfway up, she realised that she had not asked whether there were any more guests staying at the Dog & Duck or if Mr Franklin had been their only boarder. Evelyn contemplated going back down, but forced herself to forge ahead. This would be her only chance to see the body. At any moment the pub would be full of people and her opportunity would be lost.

Evelyn cautiously opened the door and peered in to the darkened room. The curtains were still pulled closed and the bed was still made. Other than those two facts, Evelyn didn't notice anything other than the body of Ernest Franklin on the floor near a small writing desk underneath the window.

Carefully she moved over to see if there was anything on the desk. A pen lay on top of the wooden surface as though someone was preparing to write something. She looked around and noticed a piece of paper underneath the table.

"Mrs Northmoor."

"Mrs Chr…that is…*Lady* Northmoor." Evelyn put as much disdain as possible into her voice as she turned around.

"You should not be here." Detective Inspector Andrews stared at her with undisguised hostility.

"I was simply checking that there was nothing that could be done for Mr Franklin."

"Are you a doctor now?"

"I am not." Evelyn moved towards the door, but he blocked her exit. "However, as you are very well aware, I once did the same job as you and I know how to check for a pulse."

"You hardly did the same job as me." He choked out a laugh. "You handed out cups of tea. You did not do any investigating and as a result you now place yourself in the middle of my cases. I have a mind to arrest you for impeding an official investigation."

Evelyn was prevented from responding by the sound of heavy footsteps on the wooden stairs. Within moments, Tommy and Teddy appeared behind the detective.

"Evelyn, you are needed downstairs, darling." Tommy put an arm around his wife and drew her out of the room.

Teddy passed by and stared at Detective Inspector Andrews. "If you could leave the room while I conduct my checks?"

"What's going on, Tommy?" Evelyn whispered as he ushered her down the stairs.

"Davey has something in his mouth that he is refusing to let go of."

Within moments they were out in the fresh air and Evelyn's heart started to slow to a more normal rate. That is, until she saw the item in Davey's mouth. The puppy proudly bounced up to his mistress and deposited the yellow, blood stained handkerchief at her feet.

Chapter Nine

When they returned from the village, Tommy and Evelyn went straight to their room. Evelyn had rarely seen her husband as upset as he was that afternoon.

"I should have done more." Tommy sat on the edge of their bed and put his head in his hands. "But I was in a hurry to do the right thing and rush back up here to the house so I wasn't late for dinner with our guests."

"What do you think you could have done differently that would have changed the outcome? You did leave him a note, what more could you have done?"

"Everything. I pushed him too hard, accused him of writing the letters, told him I knew he didn't work for the York Times. And then I just *left* him." Tommy raised tortured eyes to Evelyn. "You didn't see his face when he spoke about the Carpelli scandal. It was as though he knew the pain of the soldiers who were failed because their supplies were not up to scratch."

"Maybe he did."

"What did you say?" Tommy stared at her. "You can't mean…"

"Either he was older than we thought and was there to see comrades lose their lives because of shoddy equipment rather than at the hands of their enemies. Or he meant the word 'brothers' very literally and he lost siblings."

"And holds the people he believes accepted money from Carpelli responsible?"

"Exactly."

Tommy got up from the bed and walked over to the window. "I don't know what I think is worse. But I know I should not have left him. I backed him into a corner and instead of reaching out to me, he must have contacted the person who killed him thinking they would help him."

"You tried, Tommy." Evelyn wanted to walk over to her husband and lay her head on his shoulder and convince him he could have done no more, but his rigid stance told her now was not the right time. "You did what you could to get to the truth. Unfortunately Ernest was not ready to unburden himself. You asked Mr Hughes to keep an extra vigilant watch over things at the pub. You did everything that you could."

"And yet," Tommy murmured. "It still was not enough."

"I shall hear no more of this negative talk!" Evelyn said sharply. "Are we to work out who did this or sit under a cloak of doom and gloom regretting what we might have done or should have said or whatever?"

Tommy turned away from the window to look back at his wife. Very rarely did she use anything other than a very soft tone with him. It snapped him out of his maudlin memories and back into the present. "We are to find the murderer."

"Is that not the best way to honour Ernest's memory? Whether he was a soldier, lost siblings, or was a man who wanted to expose a national scandal. Whichever of those things he was, he deserves our very best efforts."

Tommy moved over to Evelyn and kissed the top of her head. "This is why I love you so very much. When I need someone to remind me of what is important, you do just that."

"I should hope very much that is not the only reason you love me, Tommy Christie, or our marriage is in a lot of trouble."

"Should I list the reasons?" he asked with a smile.

Evelyn raised an eyebrow at him. "The only lists we should be making right now are of the things we need to find out so we can solve this crime."

"I do like it when you get bossy, Lady Northmoor."

"And I like it best when you do as I ask," Evelyn replied tartly. "Now, are you going to remember what we need to do or are you going to write down an actual list?"

Tommy walked through to the adjoining room and retrieved a pen and paper from the bureau. Although they did have their own rooms, the only time he used his was when they dressed for dinner.

"I've noticed you have started to write things down. Are you losing your memory, old girl?"

"Your impertinence is going to land you permanently in that room." Evelyn nodded to the room Tommy had just exited. "For your information, Milly told me that she makes notes about everything and that is how she gets everything done."

"Right." Tommy sat next to Evelyn on the edge of the bed and sat with the pen poised above the paper. "What is first?"

"We need to speak to everyone about where they were last night," Evelyn said. "Specifically after dinner until breakfast this morning."

"Can we be certain of the time Ernest was killed?"

Evelyn thought for a moment. "His curtains were drawn but his bed was made. That suggests to me that he died before he retired for the evening."

"Teddy might be able to give us a more accurate timeframe but for now, I shall write between ten last night and eight this morning." Tommy wrote this down. "We know Mrs Hughes went into his room at around nine when he had not taken in his breakfast tray."

"We need to know who owns Carpelli Industries so we can try and work out if there is a connection to any of our guests. Florence is also looking into whether there were any baby girls named Isolde Newley in the York area."

"Do we still need her to do that?" Tommy wondered. "Now the vicar has told you that is definitely her name?"

"I think we should." Evelyn nodded. "Detective Inspector Andrews definitely recognised her name. Ernest was asking questions about her at the fete and then there's her odd behaviour. I have no reason to distrust what the vicar told me but that doesn't mesh with the other information we have."

Tommy tapped the end of the pen against the paper. "And after being so keen on Teddy, she then practically ignored him. You're right, she must remain on our list."

"We need to know more about Ernest. We are guessing that he wrote the letters, but we need information about his family."

"I would suggest we ask Andrews who his next of kin is so we can send a letter of condolence but after he caught you at the site of the murder, I don't think he is going to give us any information at all."

Evelyn grimaced. "No, I rather think we have used up any good humour the detective had left towards us."

"I could telephone the York Times, but I am quite certain he is not a journalist and has never worked there so that would be a waste of time. When I spoke to Teddy I suggested I might speak to the staff regarding overcoats and outer garments our guests may have brought with them."

"Write both of those things down," Evelyn said. "It cannot hurt for you to speak to someone at the York Times and it won't take up much time."

"It's a lengthy list if we are going to speak to everyone again. I wonder if the married couples will all give each other an alibi?"

"We shall soon see, my darling." Evelyn got up from the bed and put out a hand. "Now, let me check what you have written and we will get started."

"Your parents first?"

Evelyn nodded. "Definitely. I wonder if Father will say more without Mother around. There was something he was hiding last time we spoke. We must press upon him the importance of getting the whole truth. If we are to assume that the murderer left this house last night, went to the village, and managed to kill Ernest in his room without being seen by a single person then they are getting more brazen."

"And more deadly."

***

Tommy found Horace in the billiard room smoking cigars with Sidney and Frederick. He addressed the group. "Good morning. I am sure everyone is aware of the terrible incident in the village this morning."

"Terrible state of affairs," Frederick murmured through a plume of smoke.

"Hard to feel safe," Sidney added.

"It's a ghastly business," Horace blustered.

"I hope no one thinks me rude, but I would rather like to borrow my father in law for a few minutes. Family business."

Horace nodded and together the men left the room. "Family business?"

"I am certain that you agree that things have now gone too far. As Mr. Barrow said, people do not feel safe. We must act."

"We?" Horace asked as they walked down the corridor towards Tommy's office. As they entered, he saw Evelyn inside waiting for them. "Ah, we are going to do some more amateur sleuthing, are we?"

"Father, we are making strides towards catching the killer."

"I am sure the police believe they are, too." Horace countered. "Unfortunately neither one of you is working quickly enough because now there is another man lying dead who should have had years of life in front of him."

Evelyn gave herself a moment to absorb the rebuke before answering. "You are correct. We have not learned what we needed to with enough haste. However, if we were able to get the truth from everyone involved, it would be a much quicker process."

"Are you suggesting *I* have not told the truth?"

"You brought your friends here after you all received a letter. So you believed that one of the eight of you knew something. We are not accusing you specifically of being dishonest, more than there are still things that have remained unsaid."

"Now is the time to say them," Tommy said firmly. "Before anyone else is killed."

Horace sighed. "What is it you want to know?"

Tommy wanted to shake his father in law. He wanted to know *everything*! He needed to know every little thing that Horace Hamilton knew about his time as a member of parliament so he could find one of the missing pieces in the jigsaw puzzle of deceit that would allow them to uncover a cold blooded murderer who lurked in their midst.

Evelyn folded her hands in her lap and looked over at her husband. She had rarely seen him angry, he was such an easy going man, but these deaths had unsettled him. They had brought back memories of a time he would rather forget and whilst that upset him, it also made him furious as he recalled the young lives that were snuffed out on faraway battlefields.

"We need to know which of the four of you were employed in the War Office. It stands to reason that whoever was not in that department would have had little opportunity or ability to negotiate a contract for Carpelli Industries."

"This has all been thoroughly investigated." Horace lit the cigar he had brought with him from the billiard room. He blew out smoke in a long, controlled breath. Evelyn could almost see him grabbing hold of his own temper before it raced out of control. "For months we lived with the stain on our characters. Why do you think that now, with a few questions, you can find something that the official enquiry could not?"

"Just answer Evelyn's question!" Tommy slammed a hand down on the side of his desk. "While the four of you were sitting in your pristine offices in London talking about the war, some of us were actually fighting in it! Too many soldiers lost their lives because the equipment they were sent by the British Army was not up to standard. You were not there to see what misfiring guns did to soldier's hands and faces, you…"

"All of us." Horace stood at one of the windows that overlooked the driveway of the house, his back to Evelyn and Tommy. "We were all employed in the War Office."

"Now we are getting somewhere." Whilst the raw emotion had left Tommy's voice, his anger still reverberated around the room.

"Frederick and I worked in the new department that had been created following the Shell Crisis."

"Munitions?" Tommy almost spat out the word. "You procured munitions?"

"We were on a very junior level." More smoke billowed around Horace's head as it hit the window in front of him and flowed backwards to surround him like a blanket of fog. "Sidney actually visited factories as part of his role and Robert was a business advisor."

"And his role was?"

"He found businesses that were willing to stop whatever it was they were manufacturing and start making munitions for the war effort."

"No wonder you were all investigated. You had key roles." Tommy's voice was quiet but made no less of an impact than if he'd screamed the words.

"Lots of us had key roles at the time, there was a war going on. However, that does not mean that any of the four of us took bribes from Carpelli—or any other company—for their recommendation to the government."

"I asked you this before," Tommy began. "But I'm going to ask you again in light of what you have told us today: Can you think of any reason why the letter writer, who we assume to be Ernest Franklin, would believe the four of you were somehow involved?"

"That is not really the right question, in my opinion," Evelyn interjected. "It is of more importance who initially believed the four of you guilty of any wrongdoing. For it was that accusation that led to the enquiry, was it not?"

"I see what you are saying, darling." Tommy nodded. "The enquiry named four men, Ernest knew their names because of the enquiry."

"And the enquiry exonerated us!" Horace shouted. "We don't know who pointed the finger at us. Sometimes, in politics, people are accused of things they have not done so someone else is able to gain something that they might want."

"Did anyone have something to gain from the enquiry against you?"

"They might have done." Horace shrugged. "Someone might have gained favour from giving our names."

"You don't have any proof that you were set up," Tommy said resignedly.

"And there is no proof that we were not."

"Is that all you are able to offer us?"

"I have my word." Horace turned back from the window, cigar clamped in his teeth. "You have my word that I did not have any knowledge of a bribe given by Carpelli. Not back when it allegedly happened, nor now."

"I shall take your word." Tommy's words were spoken so quietly, Evelyn had to struggle to hear them.

He strode out of the office without looking back and, moments later, she heard the front door of the house bang closed with a resounding thump.

***

Evelyn didn't think her day could get any worse. She'd visited the local vicar and seen a dead body, been sorely disappointed in her father and witnessed the utter devastation of her husband.

Now she was about to face Edith Billingham—she would rather go muck out the stables than talk to the odious woman again.

She knocked briskly on the woman's bedroom door, there was no turning back now.

"Yes?" The abrupt response came from within.

"It's Lady Northmoor. May we talk?" Evelyn felt rather odd standing in the corridor shouting through the thick wood of the door in a house that was essentially her own home.

Long seconds passed before Evelyn heard a key turning and the door opening to reveal Edith Billingham. She looked about as dreadful as it was possible for a living human to look. Her skin was pale, her hair wild, and her eyes sunken in her face.

"Oh, Mrs Billingham," Evelyn breathed. "Please let me in so I may help you."

"Help me what?" Edith's voice was flat and disinterested. "Get dressed? Comb my hair?"

The widow had not shut the door in her face so Evelyn stepped into the room. The air was stale, the curtains were closed and the bedcovers rumpled. It seemed that Mrs Billingham had been still abed, despite the hour. Her breakfast tray was on a side table and did not look as though it had been touched.

"Let me ring for someone to come and take that food away." Evelyn tried not to show her distaste for the smell of the meal Edith had insisted she be served that she had allowed to waste. "Perhaps you would prefer something lighter? Shall I have Cook make you an omelette or perhaps a sandwich? A nice pot of tea?"

Evelyn pressed her lips together, aware she was babbling. What on earth had changed since the previous morning to have caused Edith to have broken down so completely?

"There is nothing you can bring for me that will make me feel better," Edith muttered, sitting back on her bed and looking as though she was preparing to get back between the sheets.

"Mrs Billingham," Evelyn said briskly, channelling her inner Milly. "Lying in bed just will not do. Sit in the chair over by the window."

To Evelyn's surprise, the woman did as she was told. Maybe there was something to be said for Milly's assertion that if you acted as though you were in charge of a situation, people invariably followed along behind you.

She decided to test her sister's theory a little bit further. She pulled the curtains open, allowing the weak October daylight to brighten the room a little. Receiving no disapproval from Edith, Evelyn opened the window a little. Picking up the tray, she deposited it in the hallway and then firmly pulled the cord next to Edith's bed to summon a maid.

"Now," Evelyn said in the same firm voice. "Let us tidy you up a little before the housemaid arrives to answer my summons."

Edith sat like a docile child whilst Evelyn brushed her hair and helped her into a robe to cover her plain white nightgown.

At the discreet tap on the door, she moved over to open it.

"Lady Northmoor!" Surprise sounded in the housemaid's voice.

"Mrs Billingham is sadly feeling quite unwell. Perhaps you could take her breakfast tray down to the kitchen and ask Cook if she has any broth she could warm through? And perhaps a bread roll? I would also appreciate a fresh pitcher of water and a pot of tea."

"Of course, Lady Northmoor, straight away." The girl performed a little bob before turning and fleeing down the corridor to carry out her mistress's instructions. Evelyn wished the junior staff didn't seem quite as terrified of her as they did. The only one able to speak to her without either turning bright red or looking as though they were facing a fate worse than death was Nora.

"Now, let me fetch a washcloth and I shall freshen you up a little while we wait for your tray."

The food arrived before Mrs Billingham had said a word. Astonished at the woman's demeanour,

Evelyn could barely believe it as Edith sat demurely and allowed Evelyn to feed her.

Evelyn was wondering what to do next when another knock on the door brought the housekeeper, Mrs Chapman, to the door.

"My Lady?"

"I don't know what is wrong with her," Evelyn whispered. "She was horrid to me yesterday and today she has allowed me to feed her lunch like a meek little lamb. I don't understand it."

"I came to see what I might be able to do to assist. It seems she has not spoken a word to anyone since late yesterday and although she has allowed the meals to be brought into her room, she has not eaten a single thing."

"I shall get Dr Mainwaring to see her immediately. Do you know if he has returned from the village?"

"I will check immediately, My Lady."

"One last thing," Evelyn said, keeping her voice low. "Do you know if anyone has told Mrs Billingham about Mr Franklin? I cannot think why that would affect her in this way, it is perhaps delayed shock following the death of her husband. I am sure Dr Mainwaring will know."

"I am certain none of the staff will have said anything to Mrs Billingham. As I understand it, no one has been to her room since they brought her breakfast tray. Perhaps one of the other ladies has visited her?"

"Yes. That is possible."

Mrs Chapman bustled off to look for Dr Mainwaring and Evelyn went back over to Edith. There was a fine line between wanting to find out answers and a measure of justice for the dead men and pushing a woman who was clearly already suffering.

"What happened to Ernest Franklin?" she asked gently.

Edith looked up at her blankly. "Who is that?"

Chapter Ten

Tommy strode out of the house and, without really thinking where he was going, headed across the lawn and towards the stream where a few short days earlier he and Evelyn had found the body of Robert Billingham.

When he arrived at the spot Nancy had sat on the riverbank and howled, Tommy turned and looked back up towards the house. Anyone approaching could be seen from the house. There was no way Billingham hadn't stood waiting for his killer and not seen him coming.

Of course, it was entirely possible that he had arranged to meet an as yet unknown person who then stabbed him to death. The alternative was that someone unexpected had met him that morning. Whichever scenario was correct, he clearly had not seen impending danger.

As he stood contemplating what may have happened to Billingham, his mind returned to the conversation with Evelyn's father. Whilst the man hadn't lied in previous discussions, he had not told the entire truth. Tommy tried to work out whether or not it mattered. Did the fact that Horace had finally admitted that all four friends worked in departments that would have given them the opportunity to procure cash from Carpelli in exchange for introduction to the minister with authority to award them a contract mean anything?

His instinct told him this was the key but he needed more information. Instead of allowing his disgust at the actions of some businessmen during the war boil over, he needed to use that emotion to focus his mind on the situation at hand. Even though he thought the phone call to the York Times was unnecessary, he would do it anyway.

Tommy headed back towards the house and was almost across the grass when he saw Frederick Barrow walking down the driveway. He stopped and waited for the other man.

"Barrow," he said, by way of greeting as he drew level.

"Morning, My Lord." Frederick gestured with his hand. "Nice walk down to the village. Posted that letter I was writing. Terrible business with that young fellow."

"Did you know him?"

"Never met him."

"I think he sent you that letter about Carpelli." Tommy deliberately kept his voice at the same pitch as the rest of their conversation, despite the gravity of his words.

"But why would he do that?" Genuine bewilderment showed in Frederick's face.

"Horace told me you worked in a government department procuring munitions for the troops." Tommy fought to keep the anger at bay as he was once again forced to remember a time that was too painful to bear.

"We did." Frederick shook his head. "But you can't think that we…"

"Of course I can think that," Tommy interjected. "Any of you could have been paid for making sure Carpelli received the contract."

"You're right, old man." Frederick clapped a hand on Tommy's back. "We could have. But *we* didn't. At least…"

"We?"

"I was going to say Horace and I didn't. We worked very closely. I would have known if he was involved in something like that. But then I suppose if you're going to do something so very underhanded for your own personal financial gain, you're probably not going to tell anyone—not even your friends, are you?"

"Are you telling me that you cannot vouch for your friends?"

"I would have happily spoken up for any of the three of them. I did, actually, during the original enquiry. And before this weekend I would have staked my life on none of them being involved. But that was before people started getting killed. Now the only thing I am certain of is that it was not me."

"I beg of you," Tommy said, no longer trying to keep the emotion from his words. "If you know *anything*...anything at all, please speak up. You cannot imagine..."

To his absolute horror, his voice broke and he had to fight against the urge to fall to his knees and sob like a child. Summoning every bit of strength he had within him, Tommy forced himself to put one foot in front of the other and then make his way up the stairs to his home.

"My Lord," Malton opened the door as Tommy reached the top step.

"Please allow me..." Frederick Barrow put a hand on Tommy's elbow.

"I'm fine now," Tommy said. "In fact I need to make a telephone call. So, if you don't mind."

Frederick looked taken back at Tommy's curt tone, but he nodded politely and walked away down the cavernous entrance hall. It probably wasn't Barrow's fault he was having to relive what he called his 'unspoken wounds', but then again maybe it was. There were many unseen enemies during the war and it was beginning to feel a little like that in his own home.

However, if there was one person he trusted implicitly it was Malton. He stood unobtrusively near the door to Tommy's office. There if he was needed, able to slip away if he was not.

"Malton, as I said to Barrow, I need to make a telephone call."

"Certainly, My Lord." Confusion showed on the butler's face.

"I would like you to stand guard, if you will?"

"Guard?"

"I do not wish to be overheard. If you see anyone approaching, I need you to ensure they do not hear my conversation. Whoever they are."

"Does that include Detective Inspector Andrews?"

"Indeed it does." Tommy inclined his head.

When all of this was over, he would give serious consideration to having the telephone moved into his office or some other private area. It really wasn't acceptable to have any type of private conversation in the hallway of his home when there was often a requirement to talk rather loudly so you could be certain you were heard at the other end.

After he had asked the operator to connect him to the York Times explained who he was, and waited an interminable length of time to get the editor on the line he wasted no time in letting the man know what he wanted.

"I am telephoning to let you know that there has been an incident involving one of your employees who was visiting this area," Tommy began, still not believing that Ernest Franklin had ever worked at the York Times, but needing an excuse to make the call. "Sadly he was found dead this morning."

After a few muttered comments about how terrible the news was, the editor's instinct for a story kicked in. "Which employee and where, exactly, are you telephoning from Lord Northmoor?"

"The deceased is named Franklin and I am calling from my home, Hessleham Hall, which is on the northeast coast fairly near to Filey."

"Franklin, you say?"

"That is correct."

"We did have a chap working for us by that name."

Tommy nearly dropped the receiver from his ear. "You did?"

"Had to let him go." Genuine regret sounded in the other man's voice. "It was terribly sad and all, but I'm running a newspaper, not a charity."

Tommy's gut churned and he knew he was not going to like what the man was about to tell him but he still had to ask the question. "May I ask what happened?"

"He spent more time at home too ill for work or sitting at his desk shaking than he did actually working. I just couldn't keep him on. No matter how sorry I felt for the fellow."

"He was suffering from shell shock?"

"I'm not a doctor so I don't rightly know. Fellow did have fingers missing on one of his hands, so that could have been why he had the shakes."

"Do you know what caused that?" Tommy felt physically ill, as though he was going to pass out.

"It happened in the war. Something wrong with his gun, I think he said."

Tommy gripped the edge of the table on which the telephone sat and breathed in deeply through his nose. Ernest Franklin wasn't missing any fingers, he was sure of it. "You said his name was Franklin?"

"Yes, Peter Franklin."

Not the same person.

And, yet, there was a reason Ernest had claimed to work at that particular newspaper. Tommy's mind recalled the words of the letter Horace had narrated. Something about his brother's blood.

"Did he have family, do you know?"

"There was a wife, some kiddies…"

"A brother? Several brothers, perhaps?"

"I couldn't tell you that, I am afraid. He was an employee, we were not friends."

Tommy could not bear to talk to the man for another second. "Thank you for your help. Good day."

He replaced the receiver, nodded at Malton and went into his office, closing the door behind him.

***

Evelyn wanted desperately to speak to Tommy after their conversation with her father but she did not want to follow him outside. Through their years of marriage, she had learned that there were times that he needed to deal with his grief and cope with the emotions he felt when remembering his time in the army by himself. When he was ready, he would find her and allow her to give him comfort.

However, that morning, every fibre of her being wanted to seek him out and pull him close to her and promise him that, somehow, everything would be alright. Together they could fight whatever barriers life threw at them—even solving this murder that currently seemed impossible.

Ann Payne was in the library when Evelyn caught up with her. She seemed to be innocently looking at the books on the shelf near the desk where Detective Inspector Andrews had set up but Evelyn couldn't be sure she had been doing that before hearing Evelyn enter the room.

Neither was it possible her actions were entirely harmless given the detective had made it very clear no one was to enter the room unless he was present. Evelyn could only hope he had been vigilant enough to put away any important papers before he was called down to the village to investigate Ernest Franklin's death.

"Mrs Payne," Evelyn greeted the other woman "I am so glad that you took me at my word and are looking for something to read. I do hope whatever you choose will keep your mind off the awful events these last few days."

Ann took her time in turning from the bookshelf to look at Evelyn. "I rather think I am going to take this one."

Evelyn looked at the book that Ann had placed on the corner of the desk. "That is a little close to home, surely?"

Ann laughed. "Reading a murder mystery is hardly going to change what is going on around me and romance novels no longer hold my attention."

"It's a very good story."

"I gave up reading romances when I realised life wasn't at all like it was painted in the pages of a book. Marrying Sidney was like a fairy tale story at first. I was Cinderella, of course." Ann closed her eyes as she reminisced. "He plucked me out of the chorus line, promised I would never have to work again, and bought me whatever clothes I wanted."

"That does sound rather romantic," Evelyn said cautiously. She had no idea where Ann was going with what she was telling her or why she was choosing to share personal anecdotes but she didn't want her to stop. There was a chance Ann knew something very important.

"It was," Ann agreed, picking up the book. "Until, bit by bit, he took away every little thing that made me who I was."

Evelyn paused, unsure of how to answer. "And that is why you don't read romance books any longer?"

"Don't believe in it." Ann shrugged. "Sidney bought all of my clothes, he decided where we would go, he chose our friends."

"He stopped you from visiting the theatre and having music in the house."

"Exactly." Ann looked at Evelyn as though trying to decide something very important. "You understand how difficult that was for me."

"I have been incredibly lucky, Mrs Payne," Evelyn told her. "My husband is the absolute opposite of what you are describing. I have no idea how I would feel if he did not allow me to enjoy the things I loved in life. Therefore I cannot say that I understand how hard your marriage has been, but I can certainly sympathise."

Evelyn tried to imagine being married to a man who would not allow her to keep her dogs or who tried to stop her interest in investigating crimes. If she suddenly announced a desire to be the next Emmeline Pankhurst, Tommy would completely support her and ask what he could do to help.

"And, of course, there were no children. Perhaps if I had been blessed with at least one child, I may not have become so embittered with life. Now I live in fear that Sidney will leave me for a younger woman and, equally, that he will not and this will be my life until I die."

"Are you telling me all of this to explain the conversation you were having with Robert Billingham on the night before he died?"

Ann smiled then and, despite the heavy layer of make up she wore Evelyn could see how genuinely attractive the woman was. She must have been quite a beauty when she was younger. "You are very perceptive, Lady Northmoor."

"I was suggesting to Robert that he should settle on a sum of money to avoid me telling the newspapers what I knew."

"With money of your own, you would then be in a position to leave Sidney?"

"That is correct."

"What is it that you know, Mrs Payne?"

"There was an evening some years ago when I had done something, I don't even remember what, that displeased Sidney." Ann ran her hands along the spine of the book. "That evening Robert came for dinner but I could not join the men as I was not fit to be seen in public."

"He hurt you?" Evelyn asked, aghast. Though given what Ann had already shared with her, she shouldn't be surprised that Sidney had resorted to physical violence when he had already gained so much control over Ann's life.

"Ordinarily he would not mar my face." Ann shrugged dismissively. "But on that occasion, there was a very noticeable mark on my cheekbone that not even heavy theatre make up could hide."

"I am so very sorry that happened to you," Evelyn told her, knowing even as she said them that words of sorrow were not enough.

"I have suffered for years at his hands," Ann explained. "That is why I was desperate enough to try and get money out of Robert."

"You didn't know what the letters referred to?"

"I did not." Ann's mouth twisted into a grimace. "But even if I did know, Robert was not going to pay me a penny."

"Did he say why?"

"Because he didn't have a penny to pay me."

"I always believed the Billinghams to be wealthy."

"They are," Ann said. "At least, *Edith* Billingham is exceedingly rich. The only way Robert was going to get money to pay any blackmailer—either me or the one that wrote the letters—was through Edith. And, as I understand it, her money is tied up in shares in her family company. She gets dividends each year which provide a comfortable life for her."

"If that is so, and I do not doubt what you are saying, then who was Robert meeting on the morning he was killed?"

"I am unable to help you there, Lady Northmoor." Ann held up the book. "Now, if you will excuse me I am going to sit somewhere quiet to read."

"If it is too painful for you to sit in the music room without being able to play, may I suggest the nursery?"

"The nursery, Lady Northmoor?"

"I can explain to you which room it is or I will have Mrs Chapman show you. She would be happy to make sure you have all that you need up there. It is on the opposite wing from the guest bedrooms and almost directly above the kitchen so it's always very warm. There's a window seat where I think you would be most comfortable."

Ann grasped Evelyn's hands. "Thank you."

Evelyn tightened her fingers around the other woman's cold ones. "You are very welcome. I hope it goes without saying that what you have told me today will remain between us."

As they moved away from the bookcase, Malton met them in the doorway. "Lady Northmoor, is everything alright?"

"It certainly is, Malton, thank you. Could you perhaps ask Mrs Chapman to show Mrs Payne to the nursery? She wishes to read a book and, unfortunately, she cannot use the library."

"Of course, Lady Northmoor." The butler inclined his head. "Lord Northmoor asked me to find you and let you know he needs to speak with you in his office."

"Do excuse me, Mrs Payne."

Evelyn hurried to meet Tommy, needing to give him the comfort he would surely require but also wanted to receive it from him. Speaking to Mrs Payne had left her feeling very sad. How dreadful it was that some women were forced to live in such unhappy marriages.

***

"Hurry, darling," Tommy urged as Evelyn entered his office.

"What is happening?"

"Florence just telephoned from London."

Evelyn shook her head. "I didn't hear it ring."

"No matter," Tommy said. "We do not have time to waste. Andrews is almost back. We need to get out of the house and into the village before he waylays us."

"He will want to speak to us about this morning, what we saw and heard."

"He most certainly will," Tommy agreed. "Now stop chinwagging and let's go."

He grabbed her hand and hurried her out of his office and down the corridor towards the kitchen.

"Tommy Christie," she gasped. "Are you making me leave via the back door."

"Indeed I am, Lady Northmoor." he chuckled. "Are you completely scandalised?"

"Enormously, but what fun."

Evelyn shouldn't have been surprised to see Doris waiting near the back door with her coat and hat. Tommy's outdoor clothes were hanging on a peg next to the door.

"Brown has brought the car round for us. As soon as we receive the signal, we will leave for the village."

"Surely Andrews will see us?"

There was only one vehicular entrance to Hessleham Hall and if the detective was currently coming up the drive, Evelyn could not understand how it would be possible for them to leave the same way.

"There will be a signal."

"That is not an answer, Tommy."

Doris giggled. "It's a quite magnificent plan, Lady Northmoor."

"Do explain."

"Well," Doris began. "I was quite busy, so Nora offered to take Davey for a walk. You know how much she loves the dogs."

"Please get to the point, Doris."

"Unfortunately Davey is going to pull on his lead at almost the exact moment that policeman gets out of his car. Nora is going to bump into him and his hat will fall to the ground. This will excite Davey so much that he will pull so hard, Nora will drop the lead and Davey will run off with the policeman's hat."

"Allowing us to drive away completely unseen." Tommy finished.

"Ingenious."

"Isn't it?" Tommy puffed out his chest proudly.

Malton appeared at the other end of the corridor. "Now, My Lord."

Evelyn hurriedly pulled on her coat, took her hat from Doris, and followed Tommy out into the waiting car.

As soon as they were settled in the back, Evelyn turned to her husband. "Now do explain to me why we have essentially run away from our own home."

"Florence telephoned with news. The line was very bad so she is going to send us a telegram."

"So we are going into the village to collect it?"

"Quite."

"*We* are going into the village to the post office to pick up a telegram?"

"I didn't want to wait for someone to bring it back to us. Better we are out of the house given Andrews will wish to speak to us."

"You are becoming rather sneaky, Tommy Christie."

He leaned over and kissed her. "Only when there is a murder to solve, my love."

When they arrived, Brown opened the door for Tommy who then walked around the car to open Evelyn's door. After helping her out of the car, he told Brown that they would be back shortly.

"Lord Northmoor!" Percy Armstrong exclaimed, startling as though he was a naughty schoolboy who had been caught doing something wrong by his teacher.

"Good morning." Tommy greeted the owner of the post office. "We are expecting a telegram. Do you have it?"

"I believe so, My Lord." Percy moved away from the counter and into the back of the post office. He quickly returned with an envelope. "Here we are."

"You are most kind."

"Where should we go to read it?" Evelyn whispered.

"There's a bench in the village green, near the war memorial. Let's sit there for a moment."

Although tragic, it was also somewhat appropriate that they sit near a monument erected to the memory of the men who had left the village to fight a war and not returned. Especially when they were hopefully going to find out information uncovering who was responsible for a scandal that caused unnecessary, extra suffering.

Tommy pulled the telegram out of the envelope and read the contents out loud. "Carpelli Industries Limited: company incorporated by Mr G Carpelli.

Directors are Mr G Carpelli and Miss Carpelli. No initial. No girls born in the York area named Isolde Newley. With love, Florence."

"What do we do now?"

Tommy's face was set in grim lines. "Now we visit your new vicar friend and insist that he accompany us back to the house to get to the bottom of Miss Newley's identity immediately. Is she, in fact, Miss Newley. Or is she Miss Carpelli. Or someone else entirely?"

Chapter Eleven

"You will stay for luncheon won't you, Vicar?" Tommy asked as they got out of the car at the front of the house.

"Am I free to leave if I choose?"

"Of course."

"Then I should love to stay," John Capes replied. "Am I to find out the reason for being rushed out of my home and spirited away up here? I was finally getting somewhere in my crossword puzzle."

"I apologise, Vicar," Evelyn said.

"It was my idea that you come here and we sort out the matter concerning Miss Newley once and for all." Tommy led them into the drawing room and asked Malton to locate Isolde and bring her to join them immediately. He then left strict instructions they were not to be disturbed.

He looked over at the drinks tray with longing. He enjoyed a drink, same as any other man, but it was most unusual that he felt the urge to take one in the middle of the day. It was a clear sign of the toll the day was taking on him.

When Isolde arrived, she looked between them all and seated herself next to Evelyn.

"It is time to come clean, Miss Newley." Tommy glared at her. "We are trying to uncover a murderer and we have wasted quite enough time being given the run around by yourself and the vicar here."

Isolde turned a faintly accusatory look at Evelyn. "I did tell you that I was not connected to what happened to that man. To either of the men. I saw

146

Dr Mainwaring a few minutes ago and he told me about the reporter."

"Who, in fact, are you then?" Tommy demanded. "Miss Newley, Miss Carpelli, or neither?"

"My name is Isolde Newley. That is not a lie."

"I did confirm that to you, Lady Northmoor."

"You did, Vicar. However, I believe I am a little late in realising what we should have asked Cousin Florence to look at in the records at Somerset House is a marriage certificate, isn't it?"

Isolde bowed her head as shame coloured her cheeks.

"I have known Mrs Newley for many years," John Capes spoke up. "In fact, I married her. Much against my better judgement, as she was aware. Unfortunately Mr. Philip Newley had always been somewhat of a rogue."

"I had hoped marriage would be the making of him," Isolde said miserably. "But, instead, he shattered my dreams and his promises over and over again."

"Where is he now?" Tommy asked, his voice still rougher than normal but not as harsh as it had been moments earlier.

"He is in prison." If possible, Isolde's cheeks heated even more.

"That is why I suggested she come here," the vicar said. "It's a quite lovely spot and I didn't think he would find her when he was released."

"That's why you were uncomfortable around Ernest Franklin, because you believed he was a journalist from York and if he reported your presence at the fete your husband may see it in the paper and would know where you were?" Evelyn asked.

"That was my fear."

"And Teddy?" Tommy snapped.

"I am very fond of Dr Mainwaring and I could not resist when Lady Northmoor suggested matchmaking. I did then try to let him down gently when I realised it would not be fair to allow him to think we could be anything but friends. But, oh, it was so very lovely to believe in the good in a person for change."

Isolde began to weep. Evelyn put an arm around her shoulder. "Do not trouble yourself, Dr Mainwaring will understand."

"I know he will," Isolde sniffed. "And that's what makes this so hard. He will see I meant no harm and he will forgive me and that will only further prove what a jolly decent fellow he is. That only reminds me that I married a man who is as dishonourable as your Dr Mainwaring is honourable."

"You were not named Isolde Carpelli before you married?"

"Grant," the vicar answered as Isolde continued to cry. "Isolde Grant. If you require proof, I can give you the name of the church in which she was christened and you may speak to the vicar there and have him verify what I say in the records."

"I shall take your word for it, Vicar." Tommy looked his way. "Though I do wish you had told us this before."

"You can see why we didn't, I hope." The vicar addressed Evelyn. "I do hope this will not change your agreement to attend church more often, my dear."

Evelyn smiled. "Not at all, Vicar. I am sure Miss Newley has appreciated having a friend such as yourself to rely on."

"Mrs Newley," Isolde said morosely. "I wonder if you would allow me to speak to Dr Mainwaring and explain myself?"

"It is none of our business," Tommy said. "I have only sought to involve myself as he is a dear friend and I did not wish to have his tender heart trifled with."

"He is very lucky to have such a good chum." Isolde plucked a handkerchief from her sleeve and dried her eyes. "I hope he will, in time, trust me enough to call me a friend."

"I will come with you to find him," Evelyn said, getting to her feet. "I must check that he has seen Mrs Billingham and see if there is anything he suggests I do for her."

"That will leave us together for a time, Lord Northmoor."

"Indeed, Vicar." Tommy looked nervously at Evelyn.

"Don't look frightened, my boy, I am a simple country vicar." John Capes smiled benignly. "We don't have to talk about anything or, if there is something bothering you, we can talk about it. Or perhaps you would prefer it if I said a prayer for you?"

"I have never really been one for religion, Vicar."

"Never too late to start. Now, while we are in private shall we perhaps cease with formalities and simply be John and Tommy? Two men together getting to know each other. If you don't wish to chat, perhaps you have a copy of today's Times? We could complete the crossword together."

Evelyn left the drawing room, happy that if Tommy wished to unburden himself he was able. She was secure enough in their marriage and his love for her to know that there were times he would rather speak to anyone but her about what he had seen during the war.

She hoped fervently he now had that person.

***

Tommy enjoyed his chat with the vicar immensely. As soon as he did as the elderly man had suggested and forgot all about religion and allowed himself to just talk to him man to man, Tommy had relaxed and found the vicar was not only very easy to talk to, but was also a thoroughly nice chap.

After luncheon when he arranged for Brown to take the vicar back to the village, he had found himself agreeing to attend church that Sunday. Wisely, John Capes had asked Tommy to examine why he was so resistant to the idea of religion, suggested he think it through, and said he would talk to him more after the service.

It left him in a more buoyant mood and feeling able to cope with facing another chat with Sidney Payne. Prior to lunch and meeting the vicar, he felt emotionally drained and ill equipped to talk to the man. Now, however, he wanted to speak to him one last time and solve the murders. Then, he would never have to entertain men such as Sidney Payne in his home ever again.

He was in the billiard room, as usual, smoking a cigar and drinking brandy. Tommy nodded at the decanter. "Bit early, isn't it?"

There was no need to dwell on the fact that only a couple of hours earlier, he had been ready to imbibe himself.

"We are rather trapped in the house, what else is there for us to do?"

Tommy stopped short of suggesting what he would like the other man to do. No need to cause a commotion when the detective was next door. "I have a few things to clarify with you. I propose we get straight to the point."

"As you wish."

"You did not tell me that your job during the war was to visit factories that were willing to stop producing their usual goods and to start making munitions."

"You did not ask."

"You and Billingham were the ones best placed to arrange for Carpelli to win a particular contract if they paid a cash incentive."

"I do not deny my particular role. I do, however, deny that I was involved as I have always done."

"You suggested when we were out riding yesterday that if Billingham were involved, he would not admit to it or pay a blackmailer. Do you stand by that?"

"I do, that was his nature."

"Even though it appears that the blackmailer himself is now dead?"

Sidney raised his eyebrows. "That journalist fellow was the blackmailer?"

"It appears so."

"Then I would suggest to you that the murderer must be someone who has more to lose than Billingham had."

"Barrow and my father in law have their reputations, their good name. You have that too, and your wife's background."

Sidney laughed then. "Anyone who has known me for any length of time is aware of Ann's work in the music halls. The only person that actually cares about things like that is Edith Billingham. You will need something more than that to throw at me."

"Your career will be at risk if this is all brought back into the public eye."

"It is publicity we could do without, I grant you that. However, we will be exonerated now as we were then because there is simply no evidence any of us did a thing wrong. There is no court in the land that can prove it."

Tommy would not admit that he knew Sidney Payne to be correct. There was no way that he could see anyone could provide the evidence necessary for the guilty party to be caught.

Unless, perhaps, it was possible for a trap to be laid for the murderer to walk right into. A plan began to form in Tommy's mind. He was going to need a lot of help to pull it off, but he knew just the people to provide that assistance.

"One last thing, Mr Payne, can you confirm where you were last night?"

"I was here, man! You know that."

"Sorry," Tommy said. "I meant after dinner. Specifically between ten last night and eight this morning?"

"I was in bed."

"Excuse my impertinence." Tommy pulled a face that he hoped did convey some sort of sorrow, though in reality he was past caring about social niceties around this repugnant man. "But were you with your wife?"

"Are you asking if I sleep in the same bed as my wife?" Sidney Payne bellowed.

"Only so far as your ability to verify her whereabouts and she yours."

"She cannot verify mine." For the first time, Sidney looked uncomfortable. "My wife regularly takes a sleeping powder. So although I can tell you that she was in her bed, she is not able to say the same about me."

Tommy nodded. "As I thought."

He left the billiard room and went immediately next door to speak with Detective Inspector Andrews. It was time to piece together the knowledge that he had and ask for the man's assistance in putting together the last piece of the puzzle.

***

As the afternoon wore on, Evelyn became more anxious. Tommy had explained his plan before he had left the house with Detective Sergeant Montgomery. Uniformed police had arrived and were guarding the entrances and exits of the house.

The ladies, apart from Edith Billingham, had gathered in the drawing room for afternoon tea which Malton had served. He now stood as unobtrusively as possible for a man to be in a room full of ladies near the door in case he was needed again.

"Will Tommy be back for dinner?" Aunt Em asked.

"I rather think not," Evelyn replied. "He has a lead on a witness that he is following up. If it comes through, we should have a resolution this evening with a bit of luck."

"Is Mrs Billingham still unwell?"

Margaret Barrow spoke up. "She allowed me to visit her earlier. The shock of Robert's death has hit her very hard. She looks as though she is on the verge of losing her mind. Dr Mainwaring has arranged for a nurse to sit with her at all times."

"How very sad," Aunt Em murmured.

"Did the police ask everyone where they were last night at the time poor Mr. Franklin was killed?" Evelyn asked.

"They asked me," Aunt Em confirmed. "I had the most terrible job convincing Detective Inspector Andrews that I hadn't climbed out of my window, popped down to the village and then strangled that poor fellow."

"Oh but that's not right." Margaret Barrow shook her head emphatically. "He was not strangled."

"Was he not?" Aunt Em asked innocently. "Do I have that wrong?"

"Quite wrong I should think," Margaret said. "There was such a lot of blood, strangling would not cause that."

"Goodness, how clever of you, Mrs Barrow." Aunt Em hung her head as though embarrassed she had the facts wrong.

"How did you know Mr Franklin was not strangled?" Evelyn asked sharply, twisting slightly in her seat so she faced the older woman directly.

She raised one shoulder in a shrug. "I do not recall. Someone must have told me."

"Who?" Evelyn fired the word so sharply, Margaret Barrow actually flinched.

"I..." The older woman stammered. "I think I may have overheard a conversation."

"'May have'?"

"Okay, yes." Margaret practically sulked at being found out. "I heard the detectives talking. They said something about your puppy finding a bloody handkerchief they thought belonged to the victim. That animal has always got something in his mouth."

"It is a shame his teeth are not sharper," Aunt Em whispered and nudged Evelyn. "Then we would never have to see that revolting neck warmer ever again."

"I didn't catch that, Lady Emily?"

"I was just saying," Aunt Em said sweetly. "How everyone needs to keep a close eye on their things if the puppy has developed a magpie complex. Goodness only knows what he may run off with next."

"Indeed." Margaret smiled at the group as though she wished to impart more knowledge. "I was able to tell the detectives that I was with my husband all night. It cannot have been either of us. We are completely innocent."

"That must be another thing I heard wrong." Aunt Em smiled mischievously. Evelyn wished she could step on the old lady's foot to stop what she was about to say. She could already tell from Em's expression it was going to be bad. "I was certain my maid was chattering on this morning about some fellow named Barrow who could not sleep last night because his wife snored quite terribly."

Fortunately Evelyn was saved from answering as the telephone sounded in the hall. Shortly thereafter, Malton announced that the call was for her and she left a stunned Margaret Barrow trying to explain to Aunt Em how she must speak to Dr Mainwaring about getting her hearing checked.

After she had taken the call, she settled back into the drawing room.

"Was that Tommy?" Aunt Em asked.

"Yes, it was." Evelyn nodded. "He said he will be home quite late this evening with his witness."

"Witness?" Margaret Barrow echoed.

"That is correct. My husband has located the fellow who saw the person took the money from Carpelli. He has identified him and he will stay here tonight and speak to the police first thing in the morning. Mrs Chapman is making a room up for him as we speak."

"Good old Tommy, I knew he would not let us down. He is such a fine young man. The police force must rue the day he inherited this title and was not able to work for them any longer."

"What do you say we have an early drink to celebrate this wonderful news?" Evelyn suggested.

"I thought you would never ask." Aunt Em signalled to Malton. "I believe it is gin and tonics all around, Malton."

"Yes, Lady Emily. At once."

Chapter Twelve

Later that evening, Tommy crawled into bed beside Evelyn. "You don't have to creep around like a mouse, I am awake."

"I was trying to be quiet."

"As if I could sleep before you were home."

"I presumed you would be tired out from all the excitement of setting things up here. Everything went smoothly?"

"Yes, Aunt Em was marvellous. As I knew she would be." Evelyn relayed to Tommy the comment his aunt had made about Margaret snoring.

He chuckled. "Was she outraged?"

"Completely. It is like having a naughty child. I have no idea what she is going to say next."

"About a child?" Tommy whispered in her ear.

"I am coming round to the idea."

Tommy kissed her cheek and pulled her into his arms. "I am so very glad. Now, let us lay here and pretend to sleep while we wait for the next murder to happen."

"He will be quite safe, won't he?"

"He's downstairs in the library with Andrews and Montgomery. There is a policeman in the bathroom of the room Mrs Chapman arranged for 'the witness'. They have arranged the bed to look as though someone is sleeping in it."

"You don't think the murderer will come after you because we were so very clear that you had worked out who it was?"

"I explored that possibility with Andrews. We came to the same conclusion."

"And that was?" Evelyn pressed him.

"That the murderer would not wish to take on two people, you and I. In addition, if they killed the witness all we would be left with is hearsay, what I had been told, whereas the witness is exactly that. An eyewitness to a crime."

"There's really nothing that we can do but wait?"

"Nothing. Have a little patience, darling."

"That alright for you to say, you have been out all day. Whereas I have been home waiting, putting your plan into action, then waiting some more."

"I am well aware how much you detest having to wait for anything but this cannot be rushed."

"I understand that," Evelyn sighed. "Maybe we should have brought Nancy upstairs, she would have barked the place down to warn us the murderer was about to strike."

"We don't want that," Tommy said. "We want the murderer to strike otherwise they could claim they had gone to the wrong room or were sleepwalking or some other excuse."

"You really have thought of everything, haven't you?" Evelyn asked with a proud note in her voice.

"Andrews and I did it together. When he's not being an arrogant ... man, he's actually a rather decent fellow."

"You would say that, fellow police officers sticking together. He was incredibly rude to me when he found me at the Dog & Duck."

"To be fair to the man, Ev, you did intrude on a crime scene. He had a right to be a little vexed."

"Goodness, you will be off solving crimes with Andrews and leaving me out next time."

"Next time?" Tommy laughed nervously. "I rather hope there isn't a next time. I must confess that I am very interested in what you said earlier. About coming around to the idea of us having a child of our own. Just imagine, we could have a baby by next Christmas."

It was Evelyn's turn to feel nervous. Her stomach knotted. It wasn't that she didn't want to have a baby with Tommy, it was the fear of how much things would change, on top of all her other worries. "Let us get used to being Lord and Lady Northmoor first, Tommy. Maybe when we have that mastered it will be time to introduce a little one into our family."

Tommy stroked her hair but didn't say anything. Evelyn could feel his disappointment and she felt guilty—as though she had handed him a present and then taken it back.

She must have dozed off because suddenly shouting and screaming filled the night air. Tommy leaped from the bed, threw open the bedroom door and rushed out into the corridor.

"Did we get him?" Evelyn heard Tommy call as he raced away from their room. It seemed an age before she had got up and thrown her wrap over her nightgown and joined her husband in the room they have given their overnight guest.

Doors opened and heads popped out along the corridor as Edith Billingham was manhandled out of the room and placed into handcuffs. A large kitchen knife lay on the floor next to her feet.

***

It was at least half an hour later before everyone was gathered together in the drawing room. Edith sat on a chair to the left of the fireplace, near the door, with a uniformed police officer standing sentinel on either side.

She had begged to be taken out of the handcuffs, particularly when her friends started coming into the room but Detective Inspector Andrews had refused. As he had pointed out, she was a very dangerous woman who had brutally killed two men. She could not be trusted out of handcuffs. Who knew what she might do when desperation had already led her to cold blooded murder.

Aunt Em sat forward on the settee, looking expectantly at Evelyn and Tommy who stood in front of the fireplace.

"May I?" he asked the detective.

"It is your home and these are your guests, Lord Northmoor," Detective Inspector Andrews replied. "Please carry on."

"As you know," Tommy began. "We became aware very quickly following Billingham's death that he and three of his friends had been sent identical letters suggesting someone knew more about the Carpelli scandal. At first, I must admit, I was quite certain that there was no new evidence and the letter was simply a ruse to obtain money."

"What changed your mind?" Aunt Em asked.

"It was the look on Ernest Franklin's face when he spoke about the Carpelli scandal. He went from being a young man in over his head to a completely broken individual. The look of pain was heartrending. He *knew*, I was certain, exactly what it was to experience some sort of loss because of shoddy equipment sent to the army by companies such as Carpelli. I just didn't know at that time what had caused his anguish."

"I must interject at this point," Andrews said. "Lord Northmoor wrote a letter to Ernest Franklin before he left the Dog & Duck asking him to either contact him here at Hessleham Hall or to send word via the local police constable."

"In all honesty," Tommy continued. "I was not sure at that point whether Ernest was in danger or the killer. However, I did want to try and keep him safe. Sadly, I am afraid, he chose to stay at the pub and unfortunately followed through plans I believe he had already made to meet up with his killer."

"Meanwhile," Evelyn took up the story. "There were a lot of other things going on that confused things greatly. We do not propose to go into any detail with regards to the personal lives of our guests, so there may be occasions when we shall move on and you will all, I hope, trust that we have investigated each person thoroughly. Our conclusions regarding the killer were made only by being able to eliminate every other person."

"Everyone did appear, at first, to have a motive," Tommy said. "As Evelyn has just pointed out, we were able to eliminate some people following investigations, such as Miss Newley. We had no evidence either way in respect of my father-in-law, Horace Hamilton, but he gave me his word he had nothing to do with Carpelli. I chose to believe him and, as time went on, we were able to officially eliminate him from the list of potential suspects."

"Because he said so?" Sidney Payne scoffed. "I told you I hadn't done anything, but you didn't believe me, did you?"

Tommy looked directly at the other man without breaking eye contact. "No, I did not believe you. But that was mostly because I did not like you. Being an unpleasant individual does not, however, make a person a criminal."

"You bloody upstart!"

"If you speak like that in front of the ladies again," Tommy said, voice low and full of steely resolve. "I shall remove you from my house immediately. I do not care that it is the middle of the night. I will remove your belongings and throw them onto the drive next to you. Are we clear?"

"I had thought you believed the murderer to be a man?" Isolde asked.

"We did," Evelyn agreed. "We had a sighting of what we were told was a man walking along the edge of the house towards the river early on the morning that Robert was killed. Of course, we now believe that was Edith disguised as a man in case she was seen."

The assembled guests looked towards Edith Billingham and her stocky shape. There was no doubt that wearing a hat and a large overcoat, she could have been mistaken for a man in the poor early morning light—particularly from behind which is how Nora and Albert had seen her.

"But why? Why would she kill her own husband?" Aunt Em wondered.

"Of course, it had to do with Carpelli," Tommy said. "That was at the centre of everything. As you know, we asked cousin Florence to find out what she could about the company. She was able to find out who incorporated the company and who the directors were from the records kept of all companies in London. We were then aware that there was a Mr, Mrs, and Miss Carpelli who were all directors."

"We were discussing Somerset House and how records of births, marriages and deaths were held there." Evelyn glanced at Isolde as she spoke. Whilst she and Tommy were keen that everyone knew how they had arrived at Edith as the culprit, she would not embarrass Isolde by speaking about her background. "We begun to think that we may have been looking at this the wrong way around. We were concentrating on the four members of parliament, the male friends, and we wondered if perhaps their wives may be the key."

"So we began trying to work out who Miss Carpelli could be," Tommy said. "As we have already alluded to, we were able to eliminate Miss Newley as Miss Carpelli. That left Mrs Payne, Mrs

Barrow and Mrs Billingham. We asked Florence to go to Somerset House and look up a marriage between a Miss Carpelli and see who she married."

Everyone again looked at Edith. "Edith Billingham."

"And to this day, Edith Billingham, nee Carpelli, receives dividends from Carpelli Industries and is the one person who would financially suffer should the scandal have surfaced once more. The likelihood is that the company would not survive a second inquiry and subsequent loss of business." Tommy paused. "I would now like to introduce you all to the missing piece of his puzzle: Peter Franklin."

"I thought he was another policeman!" Aunt Em exclaimed. "Would this be Ernest's brother?"

"Indeed." Tommy nodded. "We were not certain from the letter whether the word 'brother' was an actual sibling or a metaphorical reference. We had decided I would telephone the York Times and I nearly did not. I have made up my mind after speaking to Ernest that he was not truthful about working for the newspaper and so I thought it was a waste of time to speak to the editor."

"I encouraged him to make the call," Evelyn said. "And that is when things finally started coming together. Once we knew Peter Franklin was alive, had lost his job due to what his brother believed was the equipment supplied by Carpelli, we knew the why and then had to work out the how and the who."

"It seemed quite remarkable to me that the killer of two men could be a woman." Tommy shook his head, still disbelieving. "I think it is because Edith is a woman that she was able to meet both men and neither had any idea of what was coming until it was too late."

"But she killed her own husband," Aunt Em repeated. "Whyever would she do that?"

"Because Robert Billingham was a greedy man who would sell his own mother to save his own skin," Edith snapped. "So I arranged to meet him to talk down by the river so we could be sure we would not be overheard. None of the others ever knew it was Robert who had taken money from my father to secure the government contract, but I thought as time went on they would all suspect him—if they did not already—because of his advisory role."

"You met him by the river and stabbed him?" The detective clarified.

"I went to the kitchen, selected a knife, wore one of Robert's own coats because it would have looked rather odd for a married couple to be seen strolling along at dawn. Then I went to meet him. He knew the net was closing in on him so he suggested I take the fall for him, say he knew nothing about the transaction and take the blame completely."

"Which, of course, you refused to do?" Evelyn asked.

"I told him I would contemplate it, but we needed to discuss it further. We met and he repeated his suggestion. Once I realised how little regard he had for me, I waited until he turned away from me and plunged the knife into his back. Just as I felt he had stabbed me in the back. It was my family money we lived on all these years, my family business he dragged through the mud with his greed, and me who he expected to take the blame for his crime."

Aunt Em looked over at Peter Franklin. "My sympathies for your loss, young man."

"Thank you." He nodded, unsure of what else to say or how to act in a room full of strangers all clad in their nightwear.

"Mr Franklin worked at Carpelli before he enlisted. He saw Mr Carpelli give Robert Billingham an envelope stuffed full of cash. Billingham was greedy enough to leaf through the money as he left Carpelli's office. Obviously when the scandal broke, he put two and two together."

"I sat on the information," Peter took up the story from Tommy. "I was a lowly office boy. A pencil pusher. Why would anyone believe what I had to say over four members of parliament? During the war, I suffered an injury because the gun I was supplied with misfired. After I recovered and the war ended, I struggled to find employment because of my disability. I had no notion of making anyone pay for what happened to me. It wasn't until I lost my job, and confessed all of this to my brother, that he had the idea of making these rich men pay some money that would help me support my wife and children. That is all I wanted. Nothing more. I didn't expect anything bad to happen to our Ernest."

"You killed Ernest and then faked being overwhelmed by extreme grief?" Evelyn stared at Edith in horror. "To think I felt sorry for you."

"You must see why he had to die." Edith shook her head, but Evelyn could see it was more in sorrow for herself than for either Ernest or Peter. "I told him at the fete that I would pay, arranged to meet him in his room and you know the rest."

Tommy looked at Peter. "Perhaps you would rather not hear the rest?"

"What she did to my brother cannot be any worse for telling than it is imagining what happened in my own head."

"Edith?"

"I took a rock I found outside the pub, slipped up the back stairs as Ernest had left the door unlocked for me. I hit him as hard as I could, took his handkerchief out of his pocket and used it to wipe my hands as I left the pub."

"But Mrs Billingham has been in her room all day, she has even had a nurse with her." Ann Payne frowned. "However did she know what was going on? We spoke about the witness that was coming here tonight but she wasn't present in the drawing room for that conversation."

"That is correct," Evelyn agreed. "But you were, weren't you, Mrs Barrow?"

"I…"

"You positively pathetic creature!" Edith rounded on Margaret. "You were my eyes and ears. You thought reporting back to me the comings and goings in the house would earn my favour. Maybe you even thought I would decide we were such good chums I would pay off your equally stupid husband's debts."

"Take her away!" Tommy demanded.

The uniformed policemen escorted a struggling Edith Billingham from the drawing room.

"Well done, darlings." Aunt Em clapped her hands together. "Now, perhaps we should all have a little tipple to calm our nerves before we toddle off back to bed?"

***

In the weeks that followed, Tommy struggled with the events that had led to the death of Ernest Franklin. Peter had refused to take any money from Tommy for his family though he had allowed him to cover the cost of transporting his brother back to York and the funeral.

Whilst in York for the service, an idea had begun to form in Tommy's mind. Evelyn had spoken to Milly and the following day she had marched up to Hessleham Hall with pages full of notes.

Tommy spent the weeks leading up to Christmas travelling backwards and forwards to York, sometimes with Evelyn but usually by himself, putting what had begun as a small thought into action.

The week before Christmas, the entire family travelled by train to York for the unveiling of 'William Christie House'.

Tommy had purchased a large house and begged, pleaded, and occasionally bullied local tradesmen to transform it into a place where former soldiers down on their luck could stay.

William Christie House provided meals on an evening, and also a bed if that was required. Peter Franklin was the manager. Not only did he take care of the building, but he would use his administrative skills to write letters for soldiers applying for jobs.

"I am very proud of you," Evelyn said as she finished looking around the building. "I can scarcely believe you turned this building from a rundown wreck to this in such a short span of time."

"Your sister instructed me on how best to obtain the results I wanted. She is quite a force, you know?"

"I do know." Evelyn nodded. She looked up at the lettering above the front door. "Your uncle William would be very proud you have used his name."

"It is for cousin Billy too," Tommy said. "Peter was happy for me to use my family name rather than his. He is a very modest chap."

"You have done a marvellous thing giving men less fortunate than yourself somewhere to come."

Tommy waved a hand in the air. "I have a magnificent man to run the place. All I did was provide the money."

"Now who is being modest?"

"You're embarrassing me," Tommy muttered. "Let us go home and prepare for Christmas."

"I think I may have the perfect gift for you."

"Do I have to wait until the actual day?"

Evelyn shook her head. "No, I can give you it right now."

"Lady Northmoor, we are in public!"

"Tommy, stop teasing. I am trying to be serious."

"What is your gift, my dear?"

Evelyn pulled her husband's head closer to her own so she could whisper into his ear. "My gift to you, my very darling husband, is to let you know that I am quite ready now to be a mother to your children."

Tommy looked at Evelyn for a long moment before kissing her forehead. "That is the most perfect present I could wish for."

THE END

MURDER IN THE CHURCHYARD
COMING JANUARY 2021

When the body of Isolde Newley's husband is found in the grounds of St Augustus churchyard, suspicion falls on Isolde and everyone close to her - especially her new love interest - the dashing Dr Mainwaring.

The mystery is exacerbated by the largest snowfall seen in North Yorkshire for years. No one can get in - or out - of the village.

It will take all of Tommy & Evelyn Christie's sleuthing powers to clear their friends and find the murderer before the police arrive from York.

A Note from Catherine

Thank you very much for reading Murder at the Village Fete! I had so much fun writing this story and I very much hope you enjoyed reading it. If you did, please consider leaving a review. Not only do reviews help other readers decide if Murder at the Manor is something they might like to read but they also help me know what readers did, and did not enjoy, about my book.

If you would like to be amongst the first to know about my new releases, please join my monthly newsletter (details can be found on my website – www.catherinecoles.com).

I have also formed a Facebook group for fans of cozy mysteries. It's a place where we can chat about the books we've read, the things we like about cozies, any TV programmes in the cozy genre etc.. It is also the place where I will be sharing what I'm writing, price drops but most of all letting readers know about FREE ARCs that will be available (details can be found on my website – www.catherinecoles.com).

Catherine

Printed in Great Britain
by Amazon